HECATE

SPEED DATING WITH THE DENIZENS OF THE UNDERWORLD

BOOK SIX

ARIEL DAWN

NAUGHTY NIGHTS PRESS LLC • CANADA

Sale of this book without a front cover may be unauthorized. If this book is coverless, it may have been reported to the publisher as "unsold or destroyed" and neither the author nor the publisher may have received payment for it.

No part of this book may be adapted, stored, copied, reproduced or transmitted in any form or by any means, electronic or mechanical, including photocopying, recording, or by any information storage and retrieval system, without permission in writing from the publisher.

Thank you for respecting the hard work of this author.

HECATE

SPEED DATING WITH THE DENIZENS OF
THE UNDERWORLD
BOOK SIX

COPYRIGHT © 2022
ARIEL DAWN
ISBN: 978-1-77357-360-1
978-1-77357-361-8
PUBLISHED BY NAUGHTY NIGHTS PRESS LLC
COVER ART BY KING COVER DESIGNS

NAMES, CHARACTERS AND INCIDENTS DEPICTED
IN THIS BOOK ARE PRODUCTS OF THE AUTHOR'S
IMAGINATION OR ARE USED FICTITIOUSLY. ANY
RESEMBLANCE TO ACTUAL EVENTS, LOCALES,
ORGANIZATIONS, OR PERSONS, LIVING OR DEAD,
IS ENTIRELY COINCIDENTAL AND BEYOND THE
INTENT OF THE AUTHOR.

HECATE

HECATE

Sometimes you need to unleash the beast inside…

Cate's solitary life as a goddess is turned upside down when she agrees to attend a speed dating event with her mortal friend. When she's paired with Gunner—a shifter with an attitude—sparks fly, and she soon finds herself entangled in a fate she cannot fight. The night will not last forever, and she must find a way to set Gunner's caged spirit free.

Can Cate fulfill her duty and link her destiny with his—before time runs out?

Hecate is book six in the Speed Dating with the Denizens of the Underworld shared world, filled with badass witchy goddesses, broody shifters, and more.

CHAPTER ONE

"I PROMISE YOU it will be fun." Darcy pouted as Cate scrubbed the remains of black wax off the slate countertop.

I believe your idea of fun differs heavily from mine, Cate mused, rolling her eyes.

"It's a full moon, so you know the

place will be packed with interesting dates," Darcy pleaded as she elbowed Cate gently in her ribs. Cate flashed her heterochromic eyes skeptically at her.

"I know what phase we're in. You of all people don't have to remind me." Cate stared her down, but Darcy didn't even flinch. "Besides, a full moon is exactly the opposite of interesting. All those poor walking cucumbers, with their emotions running high..." Cate twisted her lips and raised her eyebrows.

Humans are the worst when the moon is full, and don't even get me started on the shifters.

"Just because you are Hecate, Goddess of the Moon and all that jazz, doesn't mean you can't have *a little* fun. Especially on a full moon." Darcy waggled her eyebrows as she took the textured sponge out of her friend's hand and held it above her.

Spike perked his large, black head up from his nap on the floor and Cate smiled.

"Give me back my sponge, Darcy, or I'll sick the hellhound on you." She kept her gaze cold, stoic, but Darcy knew her too well.

"If you kill me, then who will drive the van? Someone's got to take all the rescues to their new homes, and we all know how much you *love* driving into town." Darcy smiled mischievously.

True, Cate did hate going into Applewood Falls, the only town left in existence on Earth which still used payphones and had an operating

Blockbuster Video, but only because the van didn't like *her*. Every time she got behind the wheel of the damn thing, it made all sorts of strange noises, elicited awful smells, and was bound to break down at least once in the short trip from New Haven Animal Rescue, her pride and joy. Spike looked up at them with big, glossy red eyes, panting like he was nothing more than an average German Shepherd.

"You make a fair point. I'd rather see the van go before you, but that doesn't mean I'm not above torture." Cate twitched her fingers, and the sound of nails on a chalkboard rang in the air despite there being no chalkboards in sight.

"Boy you really will try anything to

get out of this." Darcy handed the sponge back with a frown.

At that moment Belle pranced in, her black fur gleaming in the candlelight glow from the array of candles spread about the cottage.

Cate's shoulders fell as she registered the frown on her friend's face.

She's just trying to help.

She's worried about you.

Cate set the sponge down and sighed.

It was humans who chased you here to begin with, Cate mused.

It was not entirely untrue. The shifters had started to break away, forming tight knit packs, and it seemed humanity itself had started to entertain themselves with false idols, the trappings of technology, and societal importance. They'd gotten angry, frustrated. Irritable, she told herself.

But it isn't humans who are keeping you here now, is it?

Cate sighed. She'd grown rather accustomed to her current way of life. Perhaps there was nothing wrong with a little respite from the dramas of humanity. But Cate knew as she looked at Darcy, resistance was truly futile. "If I go with you just this once..."

Darcy threw her arms around Cate in a hug that went well beyond worshipping. "We are going to have so much fun!" Darcy squealed.

A warm flush crept into Cate's cheeks, and she couldn't help but return the smile. For a human, Darcy was pretty damn endearing, and perhaps it wouldn't hurt to stretch her legs just this once.

She'd ventured into the forest on a dare to cross the border, which separated Cate's cottage from the human realm. A feat meant to confuse humans, who had wandered too far into her woods—and in the face of ancient wisdom and godly presence, a rather clear-headed Darcy looked right at her, unafraid, and asked if she was really a witch. The utter gall and audacity of this human, to cross the border, to be somewhat resistant to her wardings, to be so bold and stupid, actually made her smile. She'd only been a child of ten years old, but Cate knew greatness when it walked up and knocked on her door.

After all, her door was covered in a

wreath of skulls, feathers, and crystals.

"This is it, Darcy, I mean it. I'll go with you just this once, and that's it. You have to *promise* me you'll not speak of this 'going out' again for as long as you live." She said the words as sternly as she could, as Darcy held her at arms length, her blue eyes sparkling with excitement.

"If you don't meet someone at this shindig, then yes. I will leave you alone to be a creepy witch in the woods with your pets and never speak of this again." Darcy's smile reached her eyes; she looked as if she plotted the world's demise.

"I highly doubt anyone will be interested in this." Cate gestured to herself as she donned a handkerchief style grey skirt with black boots, a layered white leopard animal print top, and a grey cable knit cardigan wrapped loosely around her arms, and had fallen haphazardly in the mad kitchen cleaning session. Her dark black hair was pulled back from her face in a loose ponytail with feathers and braids interspersed. Her long silver streak fell forward, blinding her vision in her one blue eye. She tucked it back nonchalantly.

The eyes always freak them out, anyway.

Truth be told, she hadn't really cared for humans even in her goddess youth. They just didn't have the same appeal other entities, like herself, had. Humans were frightened of every little thing, always praying and seeking guidance from her or the other deities in search of meaning, or even for the most trivial of requests. Vampires, shifters, demons, and angels didn't require such reassurance. They were long past believing in higher powers because they *were* the higher power. They didn't fear death; they only feared perpetual loneliness.

Cate was no stranger to the latter, but, for the most part, she preferred it that way. Sure, she'd missed the comfort of a mortal's warmth on cold winter nights, but Spike was as big as a human and much softer. He was also quite a cuddlebug—for a hellhound, anyway.

Too many humans had come to her with their prayers, with eyes full of tears, and hearts broken by love, seeking wisdom and divine intervention. Through the years, she'd come to learn of the ills of human men, those who did not care for their lovers as they promised, did not fulfill the needs and desires of those as they claimed they would, and who turned on their professed loves for any number of reasons.

But perhaps Darcy was right. Perhaps her isolation had made her truly cynical. Perhaps it was good to see how things had progressed since she'd last crossed the border into the realm of the humans.

CHAPTER TWO

GUNNER GROANED, RUNNING his hand over his face.

God take me now, please.

"All I'm saying is maybe you're thinking about it too much. Maybe you just need to loosen up a little, get out of your fucking head, man." Cody would not give up his incessant pestering, much to Gunner's chagrin.

"I don't need to get drunk to fucking shift," Gunner grumbled.

"No, you need to get laid."

"Getting laid won't—"

"Brooding around the fucking house worrying you won't shift isn't exactly helping either."

Cody's words hit Gunner harder than he wanted. His friend was right. He'd done everything else to try and bring about his first shift; working out, prolonged lunar exposure... He even tried meditating and yoga, which Cody still seemed to find particularly funny given the size and look of him.

Thank Jesus he wasn't actually there to see anything, Gunner mused as memories of chants and super stretches filled his brain.

The fact of the matter was, if Gunner didn't make his first shift before the full moon was over—tomorrow—he would be more than just a dud shifter. He'd be a disgrace to his whole family, the Brickmans—a line of strong, pureblooded shifters.

A name supernaturals and humans feared for many reasons.

No Brickman had ever failed to shift.

Gunner slid his hands in his pockets, his fingers rubbing the moonstone talisman he kept on him at all times. To the naked eye, it was just a pretty, shiny rock, but to the Brickmans, it was the Diviner: a rod of fate, an enchanted pebble that could predict one's fated mate. It had worked for everyone in his family, thus far, and as he felt the weight of it in his palm, he had to wonder if it would work in a speed dating session.

That was what Cody was proposing.

Speed dating.

The word alone elicited another groan out of Gunner.

"If I say yes, will you shut the fuck up?"

"My lips will be sealed." Cody smiled his patented cheesy grin, the one he'd used countless times to placate Gunner's mother when they'd gotten in trouble as kids.

That cheesy grin was a bright glowing lie, but he couldn't disagree with it.

"Fine. I'll go."

***

"You've got to be fucking kidding me." Gunner sighed in exasperation as he stared up at the flickering neon sign that read *DeLux Cafe*.

"Look, I didn't name the place." Cody ran a hand through his blond hair, his eyes sparkling with amusement.

"This has to be a joke." Gunner slid his hands in his pockets, debating fleeing the scene.

A throng of very attractive women in short dresses, all long legged and tan, flitted past him as he weighed his cons. His gaze traveled up their legs, and he thought perhaps Cody may be right. Maybe he did need to have a little fun. He couldn't remember the last time he'd thought about anything but shifting, about anything but *needing* to shift, needing to fulfill his spot in the Brickman line as the next alpha.

***

Gunner's eyes roved over the crowd of people in the chilled space inside the DeLux Cafe. The singles, who milled about, all looked almost *too* attractive to be single, he thought.

The bar itself was lit up with red neon backlights, the varied bottles of alcohol stacked perfectly, streams of light filtering through them, illuminating their liquor. The rest of the room itself was divided up with tables with singular red lanterns that held candles, flames flickering off the shellacked mahogany tables; some fitted with tufted red leather booths and others with chairs that looked far too regal to be seating in a bar.

Cody swung his arm around Gunner's shoulder, his pale blue eyes bigger than saucers.

"This, my friend, is what I'm talking about." He smiled from ear to ear as he handed him a bottle. Gunner took a swig, not caring for labels. *Beer is beer,* he mused as the liquid made its way down his throat.

A disembodied voice came through the speaker system loud and clear, alerting the patrons of the night to make sure they'd filled out their name tags and forms, and reminding them the event would start in just under fifteen minutes.

That's when he saw her.

She stood off to the side, her long fingers tracing up and down her pale arms, long black nails starkly contrasted against her skin. She looked out of place next to the group of girls he'd seen before entering the bar. She wore a dark blue tank top, along with a black skirt that came down to her knees. Knee high black boots covered her legs, her long hair, jet black except for the one vibrant silvery streak in the front, hung to her waist almost.

But it was her eyes that caught him.

One green and one blue.

The crowd started to find their way to their seats, the bar erupting in chaos as the voice came over the loudspeaker once more and instructed them all the event would soon begin.

The DeLux Cafe morphed into a blur of beer and superbly attractive singles as soon as the buzzer hit, and for once Gunner's mind was not fixated on his need to shift.

Instead, he fixated on the talisman in his pocket.

CHAPTER THREE

THIS WAS A terrible idea, Cate mused as she scanned the crowded bar.

Hades leaned on the bar next to her, his dark eyes casting her a look of amusement.

"I thought you'd sworn off dating." His smooth voice all too cheerful for a god of the underworld.

Cate bristled next to him, waiting for her drink.

"Who says I'm looking for a date?" She crossed her arms as she looked at the sea of the people.

"Cate, it's speed dating. It's in the name. You don't have to lie. We all get lonely." He playfully knocked into her shoulder, and Cate rolled her eyes at him.

In the light of the bar, he looked positively menacing, like a true god of the underworld. Long, toned arms bore the hint of his definition through his fine, Italian silk suit, and his jet black hair was slicked back in quite a debonair fashion. He looked more like the actor from a terrible Netflix movie, *365* something.

"I'm perfectly fine on my own. I do not get lonely," she retorted.

"Of course not," he drawled sarcastically. "How is Spike, by the way?"

"Oh, he's just the best!" Cate's tone changed completely at the mention of her favorite hellhound, who she'd gotten from the lord of the underworld himself, as the god seemed to be one of the only people on the planet, besides Darcy, who could handle being friends with her. Knowing all about her penchant for rescues, he'd called Cate when one of his hellhounds had become gravely injured. She'd fostered Spike for only two weeks, while his leg healed, and had fallen for him: hook, line, and sinker. Hades never asked to have him back either, and she knew he never would.

The bartender served them both their drinks, and as Cate fished around in her clutch, a hand stopped her.

"I got this." Hades smiled.

Cate huffed indignantly. "I can buy my own drink."

"I know you can, but we are friends, are we not?" He raised an eyebrow at her.

Cate twisted her lips, debating how to respond, but Hades did not give her the opportunity.

"You deserve to have a little fun. So please, stow away your bitchcraft for one evening—"

"My what?" Her voice raised an octave, and Hades laughed as he threw the money on the bar.

"You are so much fun to rattle. And so easy." Hades smirked at her. "Let loose, Cate. Forget about all your troubles, and just have some fucking fun, okay? It's nice to actually see you again." He raised his glass to her.

Cate's eyes roved the room and settled on Darcy, who had apparently already become smitten with a rather nerdy looking vampire. The two were canoodling in the corner booth on the other side of the bar, completely oblivious to the rest of the world.

As much as she hated to admit it, Hades did have a point.

It wasn't that she *despised* socializing, or dating; she felt keen to be social with Darcy. She even found it somewhat easy to be friendly with some of the volunteers at New Haven, and she did rather miss hanging out with the god of the underworld like they used to before she'd moved into the woods. She'd harbored feelings once or twice toward mortals. Namely a few females, save for one very sinfully attractive male vet tech, though she didn't dare voice those feelings aloud to Darcy. The girl would never let it go and would probably push her toward the object of her affections, like you push someone off a cliff. There was nothing she hated more than having to put on a show, to act happy and sweet. *Friendly.*

She was Hecate, Goddess of the Moon and witchcraft of all things. Resting bitch face came with the territory.

"Thanks for the drink," she grumbled as she pushed herself away from the bar with her drink, some concoction Eve had dreamt up, no doubt. Eve always did have a flair for the dramatic, and the DeLux Cafe was surely dramatic in its appearance. The swirling red liquid tasted like some combination of pomegranate and apple, garnished dramatically with a lime wedge.

Hades nodded in response as he sipped his drink and turned to saunter off in the direction of an empty table. Tiny tea lights in the lanterns cast dramatic shadows on the red leather booths.

The saccharine voice resumed over the loudspeaker, telling the crowd to take their seats once more, as the next round would begin in a few minutes. Begrudgingly she obliged, plopping down in her seat, legs crossed, feigning indifference.

Just a bit longer, and this event will be over, and I can go home in peace.

The buzzer sounded, and Cate barely looked up from her glass as a rather large man lumbered into the seat, legs sprawled out as if he owned the place. He leaned his long, muscled arm on his knee, and Cate raised an eyebrow at his poor posture.

"What's your problem?" The man looked at her, and for some reason she couldn't deny the flash of fire that coursed through her.

What the hell?

"Excuse me?" She set her penetrating

gaze on this man who dared to get smart with her.

I've killed men for less.

The man sipped his drink nonchalantly.

"You're looking at me like I'm in the damn principal's office. Not a good look for speed dating," he slurred.

He's completely shitfaced, she realized.

Her blood started to boil.

See, this is why I don't socialize.

People are fucking idiots.

She noticed his eyes glowed behind the glaze of inebriation, flickering with the hint of a shifter's essence.

Shifter…

Cate felt vaguely perplexed. She was familiar with most shifters, but this one did not smell like a shifter, did not emit the aura of a shifter. Despite such things, the glow was unmistakable.

"You're a shifter." The words fell out of her mouth without warning.

The man smiled lasciviously.

"Is that what you're into?" The way his lips turned up in the corners sent a shiver down Cate's spine, and she straightened her stance, looking over this specimen of shifter who did not meet the markings of a shifter.

She felt intrigued, to say the least, but his attitude was less than desirable.

"I am into individuals who can hold their liquor, for starters," she retorted.

The man snickered. "Oh, I can hold a lot of things, sweet cheeks," he grumbled as he shifted his position.

"I believe thou doth protest too much." Cate felt her own lips turning up in a smile.

Perhaps she could have a little bit of fun, even if it wasn't everyone else's definition of fun.

"Is this your idea of flirting? Insulting me?" He ran his hand over his face, and Cate settled her gaze on his long tan fingers. The skin looked slightly weathered, as if this man spent *a* lot of time in the sun.

Cate hated the sun.

She also noted the length of his middle finger, quietly glancing from the tip of his fingernail to his wrist, an age-old trick she'd used in her youth to determine the size of one's endowment, which never really steered her wrong.

She blushed as she realized what she was doing, and the man let out a dark chuckle, his eyes glimmering with an amber glow.

BUZZZZZZZ!

Just like that, he was gone.

Instead of sitting at the next table in the circuit, he'd managed to disappear into the sea of people, like a ghost. Thor, of all people, took his seat.

"Oh hey, Cate. I didn't think this was your scene."

She did not miss the surprise in his voice. Cate searched the room for the man who'd left her speechless, the man who had her imagining the size of his—

"It's not. I didn't think it was yours either, but thank you for reminding me just why I despise these sorts of things," she drawled.

"What's this?"

Cate turned her attention back to the sullen man who dared to make idle conversation with her. As if they were mere strangers who were only first meeting in this hellhole dressed in velveteen trappings, which served rather delicious drinks. Though, it had been ages since they'd shared a rather voracious roll in the literal hay. Ages ago, when blood and sacrifice were the only things that could soothe her pain, her loneliness. Cate pushed the memories away.

I was a different person then.

The memories of her angst-ridden goddess youth were ones she wished she could forget.

Thor held a strange, opalescent stone in between his large, calloused fingers, and Cate couldn't help but feel a pulsing energy surrounding it. It was as if the stone called to her... but that would be crazy.

Without thinking, she snatched the stone from his hand, feeling an innate desire to protect it.

"Just a little crystal, nothing more," she said as she flashed him a rather arresting look, and the god had the audacity to scowl at her.

Cate picked up her clutch and made a beeline for the exit.

CHAPTER FOUR

GUNNER STUMBLED OUT the front door, the crisp air hitting his skin. He braced himself against the side of the wall, his head no doubt dizzy from the copious amount of alcohol. He slouched against the hard, cold brick of the alley, gazing up to the moon, taking in the sight of its ominous fullness.

Coming here was a bad idea.

Gunner let out a defeated grunt as he fished around in his pocket for his keys. Yet, it felt as if something else was missing. Something that should have been there...

"And just what do you think you're doing?" A smooth, cool voice broke through his stupor.

The girl from the table, the one with the two colored irises.

"None of your fucking business," he grumbled.

"Mhmm. I highly advise you to do as I say and hand those over to me." She spoke definitively, almost as if she were ordering him. No one ordered him. Not Gunner Brickman, the next alpha of the

Brickman household.

"What are you going to do if I don't, sweet cheeks?" He chuckled, his gaze settling on her figure.

Then he noticed she held something in her hand. Something she most certainly should not have her long fingers wrapped around.

The Diviner.

His family's heirloom.

A shiver ran down his body.

I will pry it from her cold hands if I have to.

"Do not test me. You will be loathe to reap the power I possess," the woman spoke.

She stood tall against the shadows of the alley, illuminated by the moonlight. Her skin almost seemed to glow. But that couldn't be right...

Perhaps the alcohol is finally getting to me.

Her dark hair blew lightly in the wind, one long silvery streak standing out almost white against the darkness, her blue and green eyes almost so very... *bright.*

No, they are glowing.

"I'd like to see you try." Gunner approached her, squaring his shoulders, feigning a menacing look despite feeling completely and utterly ill fitted for the situation. Still, if he knew how to be anything, it was to be intimidating, especially in the face of a threat.

And as long as this woman possessed his family's sacred Diviner, she fit the description of a threat.

"I believe you have something that belongs to me," he growled.

"What, this little thing?" The woman's eyes bore into his as she held up the diviner between her fingers, long black nails curled around the precious stone like the trappings of prey in an eagle's claws.

He reached his hand out to pull the stone from her grasp, and she held her free hand up with her palm pressing against his chest.

Energy coursed through his body like a shockwave.

The feeling was electrical, furious, and sought grounding through all of his nerves, boiling his blood, and left him feeling as if he were being fried alive.

Gunner clutched his chest as he

pushed through the pain, swiping for his talisman as the woman backed away.

"What in the blazes..." She looked at the stone with surprise, then back at him, her hand still resting against his chest, freezing him in place.

Their eyes met, and suddenly the world fell away. Gunner could feel an energy in his blood, a powerful energy. It begged to be set free, like a caged animal.

Wanting.

Needing.

To chase prey, to clamp its teeth down on flesh and taste blood.

To mark the one who'd awakened him.

To howl at the moon.

Within an instant the fleeting feeling

was gone, and everything went black as
Gunner collapsed.

CHAPTER FIVE

"WHAT THE HELL?" Cate froze as a surge of energy shot through her fingertips down through her center. Bright glowing ribbons of pure arcane energy found their way out through the soles of her shoes, like lightning seeks the ground. She jumped from the sensation, her consciousness spinning as she settled her gaze on the man who had collapsed in front of her.

For only a moment, she could have sworn she saw his face change shape, but not like a normal shifter changes shape, no.

It was as if the spirit inside was... stuck.

Like a caged spirit...

She blinked, reality coming back to her as she realized the man was not moving.

Cate started to panic as she knelt down in the alley, worried that somehow, someway, she'd done this.

That she was responsible.

The door swung open and Cate's pulse quickened.

"I thought you had gotten over human sacrifices, Cate."

Cate had never been so happy to see another god in her life.

"Hades! It's not... I just..." She could not find the words to speak. Hades' eyes softened a bit.

"I didn't mean to—" she stammered.

Hades' lips turned up only slightly, the ghost of a smile. He knelt next to her and placed his pale hand over top of the man's chest. To the naked human eye, it would look like nothing more than a simple Reiki practice, but to those who had the gift, or those who were inclined to be wielders of magic themselves, the dark, sapphire blue energy that emanated from Hades' hands would be more than noticeable. Especially in the dark alley as it lit up the confines of the tight space.

"He is alive, though he seems to be in some form of stasis. What exactly did you do?" Hades removed his hand from above the man's chest, and gingerly rolled him to his side.

"I... I don't know! I just came out to give him this crystal. He left it at the table, and then..."

"Crystal?" Hades slid his hand in the man's pocket. Cate watched as he pulled out the man's wallet.

"Yes, it's—" She felt her blood chill. "I just had it, I—"

"Gunner Brickman," Hades said with a surprising lilt in his voice.

"What?" Cate searched the ground frantically for the opalescent stone, but it was nowhere to be found.

"His name. Gunner J. Brickman. Scorpio. Lives over on... Valhalla Street." Hades rattled off the details of what Cate assumed to be this man... *Gunner's...* identification.

"I need to fix this," she said as she stood up.

"And how do you intend on doing that, darling?" Hades asked in amusement.

"You're going to help me move him to my car." Her voice did not waver in its command. Hades only smiled.

"Since when did you start driving?" He said, as he braced his arms around the lumbering body that had a name.

Gunner.

"Since I needed something to

transport the animals to the shelter," she grumbled as she headed toward the streetlights, Hades' footsteps following behind her. Thankfully, the speed dating event continued in full swing at the moment, which meant Cate and her companions were left to their own devices.

At least, Cate had thought so before a familiar voice struck her just as they reached the van.

"Leaving so soon?" Darcy's eyes widened as she took in the sight of Cate, Hades, and an unconscious Gunner.

"I don't have time to explain." She pushed past her friend.

"Of course you don't," Darcy responded, rolling her eyes.

"Cate, who is this mortal that dares

to challenge you?"

Cate opened the back doors of the van with much more strength than she'd intended. The van jolted from the force as Hades hefted Gunner inside.

She sighed in exasperation.

"Hades, meet Darcy... Darcy, meet Hades." She rounded the side of the van toward the driver's seat.

"Hades? Like, God of the Underworld Hades?" Darcy's voice went up nearly two octaves.

Hades smirked devilishly.

"The one and only," he responded smoothly.

"Cate, you didn't tell me—" Darcy opened the passenger door without hesitation as Hades crawled into the back with Gunner.

"There's a lot of things I've never divulged, Darcy. Don't take it personally," Cate muttered as she started the car.

"What's with the dead guy?" Darcy glanced back at Hades and Gunner, as Cate backed up rather quickly.

"He isn't dead. I would know," Hades chimed in.

"Is he always this fun at parties?" Darcy gestured behind her passenger seat.

"Darcy…"

"Is this why you didn't want to come out? Get you around a good time, some drinks, and hot guys, and you go all serial killer?"

"He's not dead!" Hades' voice went up an octave, taking on a tone Cate hadn't heard in quite a long time.

Panic.

Annoyance.

It seemed Darcy had quite the way of getting under his skin.

"I wasn't trying to hurt him, really. I was just trying to give him back his stupid rock, maybe give his drunk ass a ride home..."

"I didn't peg you for the type to take advantage of a hot drunk guy, but—"

"Oh, my word, Darcy, that is not what I was doing!" Cate sighed in exasperation.

"In the olden days, men used to throw themselves at her feet," Hades chuckled. "No alcohol needed. Just pure, unfiltered sex magic."

Cate felt her cheeks redden, and she

refused to look at Darcy.

"Hades!" she scolded him.

He had the audacity to laugh.

"I knew it!" Darcy said with a light chuckle. "It's always the quiet ones."

"Don't listen to him. His memory is shaded from the fact he hides in a fucking dungeon all day with the undead," Cate said.

Darcy let out another laugh.

"So did he pass out *before* you made your move or—"

"Oh, for the love..." Cate slammed on the brakes as the traffic light turned red, jostling everyone in the van.

A slew of curses and groans followed as she waited patiently for the light to turn green.

"You didn't have to come with me,"

she said to her passengers.

"I would be loathe to refrain from following a situation that may end in death," Hades said.

"You think I'm going to let you walk away from speed dating with an unconscious man that looks like... that... without getting the details?" Darcy shoved her playfully.

Cate rolled her eyes and sighed. The moon caught her attention once more. She felt a strange pull, an energy, coming from the back seat of the van. She turned her head, glancing at Gunner, and she felt the magnetic pull strengthening.

"Hades," she called, and he looked up at her with dark, questioning eyes.

"Yes, Cate?"

"Can you use your magic to sense other energies? Energies that aren't... alive?"

"You mean spiritual energy? Yes. Why?" He furrowed his brows at her.

"I feel an energy coming off of him but I... I can't place *what* it is."

Hades nodded, and suddenly the van was nothing but shades of green and yellow. Gunner's body glowed, but the source seemed to be coming from inside his fist. When Hades opened it, the opalescent light cast its eerie glow among the small space. Darcy let out a sound of awe.

"I believe this is the crystal you are looking for," Hades said as he plucked the stone from Gunner's hand.

CHAPTER SIX

THE MOONLIGHT WAS bright, shining like a beacon, glaring at Gunner.

I can hear voices, but I only recognize one.

That sharp tone, which carries a hint of annoyance, but also panic.

The girl from the DeLux Cafe.

The one with the glowing eyes...
What the hell?

Gunner could hear the sound of crashing, as if objects were falling all around him, but he felt strangely weighted down, as if a hand pressed on his chest. In his vision, he did not see anything falling, crashing to the ground. He only saw a wolf emerging from the moon, with glowing yellow eyes, teeth poised in a growl that to most would be quite fearsome.

But to Gunner, it only looked... badass. Majestic, even.

Gunner fixated on the wolf as it stalked closer to him. He could feel his body vibrating with energy, energy that sought an outlet.

But there is no outlet...

Gunner realized there was no way out, just as his blood heated like a pot of boiling lobsters. He longed to move, to speak. But he could not.

Why can't I move?

A loud thud drew his attention once more as reality sunk in.

All the voices clamored over one another to be heard, but yet her voice was clear as a bell.

"Fuck!" she cursed.

So Little Miss Stick Up Her Ass isn't as proper as she seems.

"It's okay, Cate; just breathe..." a woman said, her voice cautious and calming. As if she were trying to soothe an angry child.

"I am breathing!" The woman... Cate... snaps.

"I would suggest…" a man's voice echoed closely, and Gunner could feel slight vibrations beneath him.

"I did not ask for your opinion. I did not ask you to come with me in this stupid dilapidated piece of shit van!" Another thud sounded.

"It's not like it's the first time you've broken down," the soothing woman said.

Gunner could almost feel a burning in his palm, and he attempted to flex his fingers, trying desperately to move.

The burning intensified, and Gunner could feel a sort of magnetic pull, a sort of instinct he hadn't felt in all his years. As if his body just *knew*.

She's right next to me.

Cate.

Her name is Cate.

"Do you know how to fix a broken down van?" Cate's voice did not waver but he could hear the anxiety in it.

"Do I look like I dabble in automotive engineering?" The man snickered.

"Hades..." Gunner heard the annoyance in her voice, but his attention was pulled as his palm heated once more.

Hades?

Like the Greek god of death?

"Perhaps you should go ask for help." The soothing woman's voice carried a hint of amusement.

"And where, pray tell, am I going to find help at one o'clock in the morning on a shitty road on the outskirts of town?" Cate bit back.

"Perhaps you should do as the

mortals do and find a gas station." The man known as Hades suggested all too seriously.

"Unbelievable," Cate huffed. The sound of her footsteps on the pavement behind him alerted him.

She's leaving.

She's leaving me with these strangers, and I can't move, and...

A sharp, searing pain took over Gunner's body, and the wolf reared its fearsome face again. Baring its teeth, growling at Gunner, as his blood heated once more. His nerves joined in the dance of flames, as Gunner's entire body felt like it was catching fire.

Like the flames are dying to catch onto something, but there is nothing.

No kindling, no dry leaves, no nothing.

Then a startling revelation overcame him.

The Diviner…

Just before the darkness, the Diviner started to burn. In her presence, it lit up in her hand. Like a shimmering full moon. But somehow Cate held it as if it were nothing more than a fucking pebble.

Gunner had seen humans touch artifacts left by his kind, and other supernaturals. It usually didn't end well. The power within such artifacts as the Diviner tended to drive most people mad. Mortals of the regular variety, anyway. But somehow, she held it.

And in her hands it burned.

It glowed.

The wolf's eyes stared at Gunner, and suddenly they were no longer yellow and menacing, but they had shifted into a crystalline aquamarine glow. His hand warmed once more, and he could feel the energy surging against his rather large frame.

As if the energy, the spirit…

It is trapped.

The wolf is trapped within me, and he wants out.

CHAPTER SEVEN

CATE RUBBED HER arms, feeling the chill of the air, silently cursing her clothing choice. She'd foregone her thick, grey cable knit sweater, all because Darcy suggested it wasn't sexy.

As if I need a lecture on what men find appealing.

Regardless, she'd found herself more than agreeable to Darcy's opinions. It would only have been for a few hours, or so she thought. She had not intended on traipsing desolate roads in the middle of the night when she'd left.

The wind picked up slowly as she walked at a brisk pace toward the gas station they'd passed only a short time ago, moments before the car had decided to go kaput.

This is ridiculous.

This is why I prefer to keep to myself, Cate mused as she approached the empty lot. The streetlight lamps flickered ominously as the wind blew dead leaves around her ankles, and she perked up.

It was too quiet.

Eerily quiet.

Even at this hour, there should have been someone.

Anyone.

Then she heard the gentle flapping of wings, but these were not the wings of bats or small birds, no. These were much larger, and belonged to something—or rather *someone*—she hadn't seen in eons.

A lighthearted giggle sounded in the air, and Cate found herself getting more annoyed by the moment.

Of course, he'd clear out the gas station, parking lot, and likely anywhere else in radius just so he could have a damn uninterrupted tryst outside on the surface, like the playboy he was.

"Lucifer, I know you are there! Show yourself, or I will be forced to—"

But it was not the deadly fallen angel who came into her vision.

It was a woman. Long white hair, piercing blue eyes, and Cate noticed her shifter aura immediately.

What is a shifter doing with—

"Hecate, what on earth are you doing here? How did you get past my wards?" The devil himself stepped out from behind the shadows, taking his spot behind the woman.

Cate shifted her stance, already quite agitated.

"No one calls me that anymore," she said as she pushed her long dark hair over her shoulder, her silver streak blowing in the wind like a shooting star lighting up the sky.

"Pity, I always found it to be such a

fearsome name. What, pray tell, do the mortals call you now?" Lucifer smiled his brilliant white toothed smile, the very one she'd fallen victim to once and regretted immediately the morning after.

"Just Cate," she huffed.

Lucifer snickered. "So mundane," his velvety voice echoed in the air, and he slid his arm around the woman.

"Cate, this is Chloe. Chloe, this is—"

"Hecate, Goddess of the Moon. Witchcraft, and..."

"Keeper of the Wolves. But no one ever remembers that one." Lucifer smiled deviously, and Cate crossed her arms.

"I don't have time to play games. I—" She took a deep breath, fearing the words she knew she must speak. How she wished there had been anyone else, any mortal, hell even any god other than this asshole for her to ask assistance of.

Even Thor would be better.

"My car broke down, and I am in need of assistance." She stood straight and asked as politely as possible.

"Since when do you drive?" He cocked his head to the side, his expression curious.

Cate stamped her foot in annoyance.

"For fuck's sake, does it matter? Can you help me or not?" Cate could feel her blood starting to boil and the arcane energy starting to pull at her fingertips.

Lucifer just laughed.

"What do you say, Chloe? Do you feel like a little...side quest?" Cate watched as he ran his fingers up and down her arm slowly, noting the prickle of goosebumps it left on her skin.

Nice to see some people haven't changed.

"I suppose we could make a detour," Chloe answered as she let her gaze rove over Cate.

"This way," Cate spoke hurriedly as she turned on her heel, Lucifer and his newest infatuation hot on her tail.

***

Darcy's expression paled as Cate and her associates approached the van. Hades sat on the edge of the van floor, the doors open, with Gunner frozen beside him.

"Ah, Hades, how are you? It's been far too long." Lucifer cast him a smile that looked almost polite, and Cate narrowed her eyes.

"Well, this is like a bad joke," Chloe said with mild amusement as she approached the side of the van.

"What is?" Darcy asked as she took in Chloe's presence.

"Lucifer, Hades, and Hecate meeting up in a parking lot at two in the morning." Chloe let out a little giggle.

Lucifer gingerly pulled up the hood of the van, casting her a sly grin as he rolled up his shirtsleeves.

"Your humor amuses me," he said between gritted teeth.

Darcy sidled up Cate, her voice only a whisper.

"Lucifer... as in..."

"Yes. In the flesh," Cate whispered.

"Shit, Cate. How many hot gods do

you know?" Darcy's eyes sparkled in amusement.

Cate cast her friend a weary look.

"Lucifer is designed to be beautiful. He's an angel. Fallen, but—" She shrugged.

"Hades is certainly not... *hot.*" She wrinkled her nose.

"Says you," Darcy chirped as she jabbed Cate in the shoulder playfully.

"Oh, for the love, Darcy!" Cate sighed in exasperation. The idea of Darcy and Hades together... Cate could not comprehend such a thing. For one, she considered them friends, and second, she did not want to see either of them hurt. And most certainly, as it always happened with her kind, someone would inevitably end up heartbroken.

"He *is* single right? No Persephone or…" Darcy continued to pry, nevertheless, the intrigue in her voice more than prevalent.

"Darcy!" Cate's voice raised in the silent night, drawing the attention of both Chloe and Hades. The latter had the audacity to look utterly clueless. Darcy just smiled.

Cate sighed, taking in the sight of her friend's curious stare, and she could not relent.

"I'm afraid Hades is perpetually single." She twisted her lips. "Has been for over a century." Cate watched as Lucifer called forth a fiery magic to his palm, shocking the engine with a loud bang, a clash so loud and potent it rocked the van. The doors swung open, and Chloe gasped.

"What the Hell?" she said in alarm, her gaze raking over Gunner's body.

Hades raised an eyebrow. "I beg your pardon?" His eyes widened as if he suddenly understood Chloe's reaction. "Oh, don't worry about him. He's fine." Hades shrugged, looking down at Gunner.

Chloe turned to Lucifer, eyes pleading. "That's Gunner Brickman... as in the next fucking *Brickman Alpha*," she said in a panicked voice. Lucifer shocked the wires again with a loud, roaring blast of energy.

"What the hell are you doing with Gunner in the back of your van? Unconscious?" Chloe's voice was steady now, much different than only moments before. Authoritative.

Cate sighed. "It wasn't my fault. He left his stupid rock at the speed dating table and—"

"You... went *speed dating*?" Lucifer looked around the hood at Cate, his expression one of utter surprise.

"She did," Hades chimed in.

"Yes. I did," Cate snapped, casting her friend a look of warning. But it was not a look he hadn't seen before, and therefore he only shrugged.

"Well, I must check the temperature of Hell, make sure the thermostat's working." Lucifer snickered.

"Oh, fuck you—" Cate could feel her arcane energy bubbling. The Devil himself always did have a way of getting under her skin in a record amount of time.

"What rock?" Chloe asked curiously.

"This rock—" Cate produced the small moonstone in her palm, and Chloe's eyes widened.

"That's a Diviner. I haven't seen one in ages," she said as she held her hand out. "Only the old families have stuff like this... may I?"

Cate set the rock in her hand and watched as wispy tendrils of prismatic energy circled the stone, little lines of opalescent energy reaching out toward the fallen angel under the hood of her car.

It didn't seem to affect Chloe in the way it had affected her; not like when she'd touched it, anyway.

Yeah, touched it and knocked Gunner

the hell out.

"Since when does the Devil himself know how to jump start a car?" Darcy asked in awe, her blue eyes roving over him.

Hades let out a deep laugh as the car jolted once more, roaring to life.

"Darcy, didn't anyone ever tell you the devil is in the details?" He smirked.

Cate rolled her eyes.

Leave it to the god of death to tell the worst jokes in civilized history.

Cate sighed as Darcy's gaze flicked to Hades, a soft chuckle escaping her lips.

Dear God, take me now.

Lucifer wiped his hands together, taking stock in his work, the roaring engine, Cate's glare.

"That should do the trick," the

annoying prick said with a smile. "And to answer the lady's question, eternity presents much time to acquire many skills of the civilized world. Isn't that right, Hades?"

Hades nodded nonchalantly in response.

"Uh huh, could have just said you had a lot of time on your hands," Darcy answered with a smile of her own.

"Thank you," Cate murmured as she brushed past the collection of individuals and headed directly for the driver seat.

"I'm sorry, Cate, did you say something?" Lucifer's velveteen voice carried a hint of intrigue.

He rounded her side, leaning against the side mirrors. Cate could hear Darcy and Hades giggling like children in the background.

Why must everyone be so cavalier about this situation?

He raised his eyebrow at her playfully.

Cate stared straight through the windshield.

"Lucifer…"

"Engaging in some sorcery this evening, my dear witch?" His lips perked up in amusement. If there was anything Lucifer loved more than his trysts, it was information. Gossip. Secrets, in which he could lord over you, to get you to do whatever it is he wanted you to do.

"None of your business," Cate brushed him off.

"Mhmm. For what it is worth, it was

rather nice to see you again, Cate. Do take care. Mortals are rather delicate."

Cate gripped the steering wheel and cast him a glare. She knew what he was waiting for.

"Thank you," she said with an abundance of overcompensating confidence, enunciating the words vividly. The disdain in her voice was not well hidden.

Lucifer flashed a perfect mega-watt smile and nodded in return.

"You are so very welcome." His words were saccharine as he gave a good tap on her door handle. "Until we meet again, under better circumstances, of course," he said with perfect inflection.

Hades shut the doors, and Cate didn't even wait to take off, leaving the angel and his shifter in the dust.

She sighed as she focused ahead on the road.

It's going to be a long night.

CHAPTER EIGHT

THE GOD OF death and Darcy stood in the doorway of Cate's humble abode with concerned looks on their faces, as if she herself was a teenager being left home alone for the first time.

"Are you sure you don't want us to stay? Maybe we can help..." Darcy pleaded.

Cate looked to her kitchen table, which boasted the rather large shifter, before looking back at her friends. Though she appreciated the offer, the gesture one that left her feeling genuinely thankful for the two individuals she called friends, she knew things would likely run smoother if there was not a small crowd huddled around Gunner when he would inevitably wake.

"There is nothing you can do that you have not already done." She forced a smile.

Hades looked her over speculatively. "I would say we should do this again sometime Cate, but—"

"I know. All things considered, it was kind of nice to see you again." Her smile lifted only a fraction. She had not realized how much she'd missed the company of her friend.

Hades smirked at her in favor.

"I'll be back to check on you in the morning," Darcy yawned.

"Of course. I wouldn't expect any less." Cate sighed.

She'd learned early in their friendship it was pointless to argue with Darcy. The woman always took the bait, hook, line, and sinker and would not rest until she'd had the last word. She also knew how the mortal liked her sleep, and thus she knew the chances of Darcy's morning arrival would be far more unlikely than she professed it would be.

Cate shut the door on her friends quickly, if only to get them off her doorstep faster. She needed to think, to research. To gather her thoughts, and whatever else she might need to bring Gunner back into the conscious world.

Then I will give him his stupid rock, he can leave, and I can forget this whole ordeal.

Even as Cate thought the words, it seemed a strange feeling pooled in her gut, one she hadn't felt in ages. Cate pushed it away like a pesky moth.

Keeper of the Wolves.

Lucifer had spoken aloud her former nickname, one she had not thought about in far too long. It had been quite some time since she'd mingled with shifters. It seemed as civilizations progressed, the shifters had evolved into managing their own packs, and most saw themselves as supernatural beings higher on the food chain. As the years droned on by, Alphas shunned the Keeper of the Wolves. Aside from the stray caged spirit or any magically inclined issues, they no longer seemed to need her.

They did not pray to her or seek guidance. Instead, they'd cast a bubble about their community, their kind.

But she preferred the isolation, as it were, so she did not resist their rejection.

Cate removed her shoes, tossing the boots aside with enough force they hit the leg of the wooden chair with a clunk. She set about pulling out her journals, not quite sure what she was looking for but knowing she would find an answer nonetheless.

Belle trotted out from Lord knows where, her bright green eyes looking over Cate with burgeoning curiosity.

"Don't look at me like that," Cate mused as she opened her cupboards, fingers searching for basic ingredients.

Belle only snuffed her head to the side and paraded on by. Cate glanced at the clock. How it was only one-thirty in the morning was beyond her. It felt as if the night was positively endless.

After a good twenty minutes of scuttling about her house, she'd assembled a variety of tools and ingredients she felt confident would be just the thing to bring Gunner out of stasis, as Hades had called it.

Then we can rectify this situation *and*

ARIEL DAWN

I can get back to my life...

Cate lit her black candles, holding them over her subject rather eerily, the wax pouring over the side in long, tenuous drips onto Gunner's chest. He did not even flinch, a sure sign his stasis was quite deep. As she set the candles aside, she collected her rose and patchouli oil, which was a mixture of oil and crushed rose hips she had muddled together in a smooth, marbled mortar and pestle dish. She wet her fingers with the sweet smelling oil, letting it run along her fingertips, and she took a deep breath. She rather loved the smell of rose and patchouli, the earthy tones quite soothing to her soul.

Her long fingers drew slick sigils on top of Gunner's well-defined chest, long black nails sliding through his dark chest hair, curving around the edges of his pectoral muscle. His body was still warm to her touch and heated the oil instantly.

Cate swallowed momentarily at the realization that he was the first man she'd ever brought into her cabin.

And he is unconscious, so what does that say about you, Cate? She chastised herself as she ran her fingers down his sides, feeling the muscles carved beneath his skin hard and warm and...

Cate suddenly felt rather warm herself, despite the fact she was only wearing a tank top and a skirt.

"Get a grip on yourself, he's just a man. You've had plenty of them in your time. This one's no different..." She spoke aloud to the empty room as she wiped off her oiled fingers with a damp cloth. Belle meowed in the distance, in protest.

But even as she said the words, Cate knew they were a lie.

This one *was* different, although she couldn't understand *how* exactly.

As she ground the leaves, spices, flower petals, and sacred oils in the mortar dish once more, she noticed the glowing light of the moonstone in the corner of her eye.

Belle swatted at it with her paws, pushing it back and forth.

"Belle, leave that alone!" she quickly abandoned her bowl to shoo her cat away from the precious... *Diviner.*

Chloe had known exactly what it was,

and Cate sighed in exasperation. She wished she would have asked Chloe more questions had she not been so... so...

Flustered?

In all her years dealing with the shifters, she'd never seen such an artifact, though Chloe was quite familiar with it, enough to know what it was, and she was most intrigued.

Cate sprinkled the dried herb mixture across Gunner's chest, above the oil sigil. Tiny streams of oil ran over the sides of his body, pooling against his skin, soaking the wood of her kitchen table, the herbs sparkling like glitter in the eerie candlelight.

Cate braced herself as she started to speak the words she'd thought she'd forgotten, but it was like riding a bicycle. Though she hadn't cast an awakening spell on anyone, let alone a shifter, in eons, the words came back to her almost instantly. As she spouted them, the room began to feel hot, and faint tremors started to vibrate the floors and the cabinets. Spike stood at attention and Belle meowed in protest once again at the sudden ruckus, but Cate kept going.

Gunner's body started to feel warmer, and the pull to the Diviner was almost magnetic. Cate grabbed the moonstone, twirling it in her fingers. Its glow danced in tiny wisps around her fingers, and she closed her eyes.

The words came so easily, and she did not fight them.

With her spare hand, she slid it

across his solid chest and placed it over his heart.

The rain fell quickly without warning, but she did not stop.

She could not stop.

She felt... compelled. Compelled to save this man, to free his caged spirit. As if it were her duty, her purpose. She hadn't felt such things in so long, and the feeling was more than seductive.

To be wanted, needed.

But such thoughts were silly, meaningless to a goddess who'd lived so much longer than most.

Cate could feel Gunner's wolf, the spirit within, separated only by a layer of flesh and blood. It called to her, begging for more, its energy louder than any spoken voice.

She repeated the words, over and over, and each time the draw of the stone, the magnetic pull she felt to look at *him*—this specimen of shifter she'd brought into her humble abode—only magnified.

The room continued to shake as the spirit wrestled above Gunner's body, but it struggled still, unable to right itself.

Just when Cate had thought the end was nigh, and Gunner would not return to the land of the living, her body was met by full force as thunder crashed outside, and a hand reached out for her throat.

CHAPTER NINE

GUNNER STARED UP at the yellow-eyed wolf from beneath its grasp.

The glowing white wolf reared its teeth, a low growl emanating from its depths, but he was startlingly aware there were no actual depths, for the wolf was nothing but energy, spirit.

Like a ghost of sorts.

An angry spirit, as luck would have it.

He pushed against the vengeful spirit with all his might. Harder and harder against the darkness, little wisps of fur dissipating like smoke as he pushed forward through it all.

The growls grew louder, but Gunner did not care.

There was something he needed to get back to...

No, someone.

The tether of the otherworld called to him, the familiar energy one he'd felt all throughout his life.

The energy of the Diviner.

Its iridescent energy sparkled in the dark like a star, and it called him home.

But when Gunner awakened, he was

not *home.* And it seemed he was under attack.

His hand reached out involuntarily, wrapping around the throat of his attacker.

"The fuck... are you doing?" The voice that spoke sounded familiar, although Gunner could not place where he'd heard it. His eyesight blurred in and out, white spots dancing in his vision, but he did not let go.

"Where am I? Who are—"

"Oh, for Heaven's sake..." The voice choked and within seconds Gunner felt a shocking energy against the back of his hand, and he seized his hand back.

"The fuck—"

"Yes, I forgot about the disorientation, it seems. Very well, then." The voice was low, sultry.

Somewhat hypnotic.

Gunner pinched the bridge of his nose, trying desperately to acclimate to his surroundings, which he could not see clearly. His head pounded, and the feeling left him rather vulnerable, and if there was anything Gunner tried to avoid like the plague, it was to appear weak and flawed.

A hand touched his shoulder, sending a shockwave through him once more.

"Fucking hell!" He jumped in response.

"If you sit still, perhaps I can actually *help* you," the sultry voice grumbled. A soft hand touched him once more, and this time the shock gave way to a rather soothing vibration through his tense muscles.

He opened his eyes once more and his vision started to clear. He settled his gaze on the woman in question, on the hand that touched his shoulder.

The first thing he noticed was her wrist—the underside of it to be exact. As she reached her hand out, fingers brushing his temples, long nails tracing his skin lightly, he noted the underside of her wrist bore a black crescent moon tattoo. Her skin was pale, almost unnaturally white, and in the candlelit glow of wherever they were, it looked as if it were smooth as pure marble.

Without thinking, he wrapped his fingers around her wrist, brushing the shape of the moon with his thumb. She felt smooth and slightly chilled. Like the air on a crisp, fall night.

It was her turn to jump, and Gunner noted a slight flush to her cheeks.

Suddenly the buzzing energy of the Diviner was loud in his ears, and the shockwave that coursed through his body as he touched her skin brought the memories back tenfold.

The woman from the speed dating party.

The one with the two colored eyes and the silver streak.

The one with the attitude.

Gunner dropped his hand and shifted backward, almost upending himself off the table.

"Wait... You're the girl from the speed dating thing... The one—"

"Ah, there it is. Memories are still intact, I see, which is good. Means whatever I did does not have a long-term effect. At least, I don't think it does." She pulled away from him and walked off toward the... kitchen?

"Where the hell did you take me?" he growled as he stood, looking around the room for any sign that might tell him who this woman was and where exactly he had been taken. His gaze settled on the woman who stood in a black tank top and grey skirt against a muted greyish wooden counter. The counter itself was lined with glass canisters, nearly two rows of them, filled to the brim but left unlabeled. Gunner watched as she poured a glass of some kind of liquid into what looked like a black wine tumbler with white stars.

"Why, I took you home, of course. I couldn't very well revive your ass out of stasis otherwise," she bit out and then sipped her drink.

Before Gunner could speak, he felt a large nudge against his knee, and he noted the scent of fire and brimstone clear in his senses.

He looked to his side to see a rather large black creature that *resembled* a wolf, but as a shifter Gunner was more than capable of sensing a creature like himself, or the animal within.

This animal was neither of those things, and the moment he realized what the creature was, he nearly leapt out of his skin.

He'd heard tales of hellhounds, but

he didn't think they were real.

As if the creature could sense his apprehension, it growled.

"Do you mind?" he said to it as he slowly moved away from the big black dog-like creature.

"Oh, don't mind Spike. He's harmless, really. Well, unless you are a soul bound for Hell, naturally."

"What?" Gunner's voice escalated an octave, much to his dismay. Not much frightened him, but he had to admit he did not want to end up downstairs well before his time. He backed away slowly from the creature, who just cocked its head at him as if he were nothing more than a rogue raccoon in the house.

"Why did you bring me back here? You one of those crazy chicks who want to sacrifice me to the gods or some shit?" He crossed his large arms.

She glanced over his form, before meeting his eyes.

"First off, I don't partake in human sacrifice anymore. I was… going through a difficult time then. Second, even if I *did* want to sacrifice you, it would be for my own pleasure. I do not serve the gods. Such a thing is quite pointless when you *are* one."

She said the words deadpan and it took a moment for them to hit Gunner completely.

"You could have just said you're crazy."

All the hot ones usually are, Gunner.

You know that from experience.

"I can be that, too, if you give me

reason to be." The way in which she said the words was not simple, clear. Her voice also carried a seriousness that Gunner felt to his soul.

The spirit within him responded to her voice, to her tone, and rattled against him. Gunner clutched his chest, his eyes closing as he grimaced involuntarily, stifling a grunt.

When he opened his eyes, he saw the woman standing in front of him, and she held out a second tumbler, a black one with little white moons on it, to him.

An offering.

"How do I know this isn't poison?" He raised an eyebrow at her.

"You will just have to trust me, Gunner."

Hearing his name on her tongue

stirred his wolf once more, and the beast surged forth again. He gritted his teeth but fought against closing his eyes and showing any sign of pain.

If what she says is true...

Gunner did not want to believe he was in the presence of anything other than an attractive crazy girl he'd met at the DeLux Cafe. But something inside of him knew when she'd said the words, insinuated she was more than human, more than just your run of the mill supernatural, it was true. He grabbed the tumbler from her, his fingers brushing hers slightly, the tiny shockwaves jolting through him once more. He took a rather impolite swig of the cocktail, which tasted like bitter licorice. He'd never been in the presence of a god before, especially ones offering him drinks in a reclusive cabin in the middle of God knows where. "Do I have a choice?" His eyes flicked to the tumbler in his hand before catching hers once more.

It was a strange and unsettling sight, the duality of her jewel toned irises. Pale blue set against a deep green.

Like the sky above the forest trees.

He did not miss her gaze drifting down to his lips, or the way in which her dark hair fell over her pale shoulder, the silver streak standing out against its contrast like a comet in the night sky. The round curve of her breasts, smoothed by the ribbed tank top she wore, provided quite a welcome view.

"You always have a choice," she said,

her voice barely a whisper, swallowing her nerves quite visibly. Gunner could feel her apprehension.

What reason does she have to be nervous?

She's not the one who woke up in a fucking cabin God knows where...

The spark from their shared touch rattled his wolf once more, and his spirit surged against his insides. This time, Gunner could not prevent the grimace of pain on his face as it did so.

"Fuck..." he hissed through his teeth.

Soft hands settled on the sides of his arm, and the goddess pushed and pulled him, as if looking for something.

"How long has your spirit been caged?" she asked in a tone that was all business. No more sultry whispers.

"What?" He closed his eyes and tried to push back against his inner spirit, the one who up until this night had remained rather docile and quiet.

"Your spirit. How long has it been caged? When was the last time you shifted?" She grabbed his neck, turning his head to the side. She inspected him closely.

What she was looking for he wasn't certain, and he couldn't deny even though he knew he should be on the defense, ready to attack just in case this crazy bitch went off the rails, he couldn't fight the truth—her touch *soothed* his spirit, even if it was only minimal.

Or that the feel of her nails against his throat caused his cock to twitch.

This is not the time, buddy.

Gunner sucked in a deep breath. He didn't know this woman from Adam, and divulging such personal information to a woman he'd just met—every part of it should have felt wrong. For some reason or another, he trusted this woman.

Somewhere deep in his bones, he knew she would not harm him.

Not unless he wanted her to.

The thought was startling, and it took him a moment to catch his bearings and respond.

"What is your name, again?" He swallowed. They weren't the words he'd intended on speaking, but something about the proximity of this woman, the spark in his blood, the hungry wolf inside—all of those things propelled him to ask the question.

He *needed* to know.

The innate desire within drove him toward seeking out the answer.

"You can call me Cate," she said as she looked up at him once more, her hand resting on his bicep, long nails cool against his warm flesh.

Reflexively, he reached out and brushed a strand of hair behind her ear. She stood still as a statue, and his inner wolf pushed against him once more, hungry, starving for something he could not quite put his finger on.

A strange sort of tension formed between them as Gunner stared into Cate's eyes as the sound of her breathing became slightly deeper.

Gunner forced himself to blink, to look away from her hypnotic eyes.

"Always. I have been like this, always." His voice was steady, but it carried all the pain and all the sorrow from his life in it.

It was a simple statement, but buried in its simplicity was a thousand unsaid words, hopes and frustrations that mixed together to create what Gunner had assumed would be his shameful fate.

The anger in his voice was palpable. No matter how hard he tried he could not shift.

He could not do what he was simply born to do.

Cate gasped as she pulled her hand from his arm, and Gunner noted the ache from his wolf at the absence of her touch. Such things were shocking to him, the overwhelming knowledge within that he could trust this Cate with something so personal. It did not make sense.

"You have *never* shifted?" she said in disbelief.

Gunner sighed deeply. The surprised tone was one he'd heard throughout his life from varied sources, one he had grown a rather thick skin for.

"No, Cate. I have not."

CHAPTER TEN

IN ALL THE years Cate had been alive, she thought she'd heard it all. But Gunner's words left her feeling an emotion she hadn't felt in eons.

Surprise.

It was hard for her to see the specimen in front of her—his golden chest still slick with oil, defined abs more prominent from the harsh shadows of candlelight, dark hair falling in his eyes, shading his smooth skin—as anything but the epitome of a perfect, textbook shifter. Everything about this man gave off an Alpha vibe, but yet...

He had *never* shifted.

Despite his admission, she could sense what lay hidden beneath his surface. His wolf had been caged his entire life.

How daunting that must be.

Cate trailed her fingers down his arm mindlessly as she racked her brain for some sort of answer.

She'd never met a shifter in all her years who had failed to transition. Most of those whose spirits had become caged within had already gone through their first transition.

Not to mention she knew the older a shifter got, the harder such a transition would be.

"How old *are* you?" Cate asked curiously.

Gunner swallowed but he did not take his eyes off of her.

"Thirty-one."

Older than I thought.

Well past the normal age range of transition.

Although Cate could not deny he looked rather good for his age.

Focus, Cate!

She twisted her lips in thought. A steady stream of moonlight poured through her windows, sparking an idea.

Moonlight... the full moon... of course!

Channeling the power of the moon mixed with the ritual of setting free a caged spirit—

"I have an idea," she said as she broke his gaze and pulled her hand away.

She left Gunner standing by the table as she padded around her kitchen once more, opening and shutting cupboards in haste. She did not wait for him to answer her. Belle meowed in the distance, opinionated as ever. Instead, she just started rambling, trying to piece the puzzle together.

The power of the moon, some ceremonial oil...

What was that chant?

"I used to be quite familiar with

shifters, actually. I've seen my fair share of caged spirits, but usually it was something that happened during the first transition. Difficulty assimilating spirits and all," she started as she pulled down two boxes and set them on the counter.

"Wait, you think you can actually help me? With my..."

"Caged spirit. Yes, I do," she answered with conviction.

"Caged spirit..." he repeated the words slowly.

Gunner watched her as she reached the tips of her fingers toward the top shelf she could barely reach.

"Coming up a little short there, Cate?" He snickered as he walked over to the counter. Even on her toes she only came up to his chest, and as he leaned above her, she caught a drift of his natural scent.

He smells like the forest...

The scent was most *arousing* to her senses, and she did not miss how it made her stomach flip.

He brought down the jar she'd barely been able to reach.

"Is this what you were looking for?" He raised an eyebrow, his lips curving into a smirk that made her feel strangely flushed.

Cate pried it from his hands, feeling strangely self-conscious. Flirting was never really her strong suit.

"I could have gotten it myself, thank you very much."

"So modest." He flashed an annoyed

smile at her, and she felt her stomach flip, as if she were a mere teenage mortal with a crush, not at all something she expected from the attractive shirtless man in her kitchen in the middle of the night. She huffed in response.

"If this is to work properly, you will need to do as I say. Do you understand?" She popped the lid off the jar, and the scent of stale, dried herbs hit her like a mushroom cloud.

"That depends on what you tell me to do, sweet cheeks." Gunner's cocky tone made Cate half consider incinerating him instead.

"First and foremost, do not call me sweet cheeks."

"Or what? What are you going to do if I don't listen?" He smiled back at her, the sight all too appealing.

He's enjoying this...

"Are you still drunk? What part of *vengeful goddess* did your tiny brain not process?"

She scowled at him as she crushed up the dried lavender and wolfsbane into a powder.

"Unfortunately, no. Whatever you did to me wiped the half decent buzz I had right out of my damn system."

She could hear him walking around, looking at her things. The knowledge put her on edge.

Aside from Darcy's regular visits, Cate didn't allow anyone of the mortal variety into her home. For starters, her cabin was full of kitchen witchery and prized artifacts, the sorts of things that usually set average Joes on edge. Accursed items, a prized collection of ancient animal bones she'd used for years as runes, not to mention the oversized concept paintings that were as beautiful as they were bloody. Her natural penchant for dark, rich jewel tones and skulls was not the most warm and cozy aesthetic.

No, the only visitor Cate saw was her friend, and the occasional rescue she'd brought home from the animal rescue when they were in need of twenty-four hour care.

When she heard a clanging, she turned abruptly to see one of her statues on the floor in pieces.

"For fuck's sake, didn't your mother raise you not to touch other people's things without asking fucking permission?" She set her tools down as she hurried over to the broken statue. Belle rubbed her lithe body along Cate's legs as she bent down to clean up the mess.

Gunner looked like a deer caught in headlights. "It was the cat!"

"My darling Belle knows better. Clearly, you do not," she grumbled as she swept the tiny pieces of marble into her hand. "Blaming it on the poor defenseless animal," she tutted as Belle meowed adoringly.

Gunner shifted his weight, the look on his face perplexed. He seemed to be struggling with his words, and a part of Cate was rather happy at that notion.

Good.

Let him stew in his embarrassment.

Cate carried the dust and debris to the kitchen trash swiftly, washing her hands once more in the sink. The potent smell of lavender soap perfuming the air was almost relaxing. She dried her hands with haste and resumed her herb crushing.

"Don't talk to me like I'm a fucking child."

She could feel him, his energy behind her, closing in on her space. She turned around, her shoulders tensing as she gripped the counter behind her. Even though she only came up to his chest, she didn't let that stop her from putting his indignant ass in his place.

"Don't fucking act like one." She could feel the sparks forming at her fingertips as she gazed up at Gunner's dark eyes with fire.

Something about this man just makes me so….

"You know what, *sweet cheeks*? I don't need your help." He leaned into her space, his voice a low growl that sent a shiver up her spine.

But it was not a shiver of fear. Cate pushed the thoughts threatening to permeate her otherwise confident stance away. Despite the irritable tone in his voice, his close proximity, something stirred beneath her skin, beneath her blood as Gunner looked in her eyes. Something both dangerous and inviting, something that caused Cate to shift her weight and push back.

"Fine by me," she bit back as she slid

underneath his arms and walked with haste toward the door, trying to escape the sudden onslaught of emotion she was not expecting.

It's better this way, you know that.

You don't need an unappreciative, stupid—

"Where the hell is my shirt?" Gunner's voice elevated, the frustration in his tone evident.

"If you insist that you don't need my help setting your caged spirit free, you certainly don't need my help in locating your clothing," Cate said haughtily as she flicked her hair over her shoulder. Spike perked his head up in interest, looking from Cate to Gunner expectantly.

"Just answer the damn question," he

grumbled.

"If you made the effort to actually look—" She pointed to the kitchen chair behind him, and Gunner scowled as he grabbed his shirt. Cate held the door open. The moonlight hit her skin, and she felt the sparks flare into full blown energy around her arms, blue light crackling like lightning, surrounding her pale arms all the way up to her shoulder.

Cate watched as Gunner threw his shirt on, hurriedly setting to fasten the buttons on his collar, and then he stopped. As if stasis had returned, freezing him in time. His buttons left untouched, the expanse of his chest visible still. His eyes widened at the sight before him, at *her,* and suddenly he lurched forward. Visible tendrils of yellow and green danced just above his skin, and the wolf inside him rattled against its cage once more.

CHAPTER ELEVEN

GUNNER GRABBED THE moonstone Diviner.

Fucking hell.

The onslaught of his wolf as it tried to push through him was a new kind of pain he hadn't yet experienced.

Because it wasn't anger or frustration

he felt, it was *need.*

His wolf needed *her.*

Gunner felt it in his bones. The realization was most unexpected. Especially given the fact he'd just threatened to walk out.

The reality was undeniable.

The fractals dancing up and down her arm seemed to have awakened his wolf, and the feeling left his entire body alive with shifting energy. Shifting energy he'd never felt so strongly before.

His body *begged* to shift, and the images that flashed in his brain were both startling and alarming.

Every part of him moved of its own accord, and suddenly Gunner found himself on the precipice of Cate's doorstep, boxing her against the wooden door.

He leaned over her, his glowing eyes taking her in like she was nothing more than prey.

But both he and his wolf knew she was *anything* but prey.

She was a goddess, pure and simple, and her magic was exactly what he needed to be set free.

"Do you feel that?" His words were in his voice, but somehow it was as if they did not belong to him.

Cate looked up at him with fire in her eyes, her beautiful dual-toned irises radiating with their own glow.

"Feel what?" she said solidly, as if he was not brimming with an overabundance of feeling, pain, and shifting energy like some ticking time bomb.

His wolf lurched forth again, and his chest ached from the push. It felt as if his bones could not take any more.

Cate placed a single hand on his exposed chest, her eyes glowing like bioluminescent algae on the lake he'd loved as a child, something stunning, beautiful even, but only in the dark did it come alive.

When she touched him this time, there was no magical zap, no shock to knock him unconscious.

Only the feel of her soft skin against his and the maddening need.

And he could not fight it.

He could not fight her or the invisible tether, or the feeling of the Diviner warm in his hand, telling him what he could barely comprehend.

With his free hand, Gunner grabbed her by the hips with force, and crushed his lips to hers without thinking twice about it.

The sane part of his brain, which seemed to take a backseat to his newly awakened *caged spirit*, rationalized that this was just not right. None of it made any sense. Feeling the overwhelming spirit within rising to the surface, controlling his movements.

For starters, he barely knew Cate yet she seemed to have a way of getting under his skin. It was as if he was being puppeted, but yet, somehow, it all felt undeniably right.

The feel of her lips against his, her energy and how it *called to him.*

Especially when Cate returned his kiss with adamant hunger. She parted her lips, her tongue seeking his in a rushed, raw sort of way that felt more animal than human. Her fingers snaked up his chest, around his neck, finding the edges of his hair, and she pulled him closer, moaning into his mouth with satisfaction. The sound alone was like music to his ears, and his cock strained against his jeans, begging to be free. Her breasts brushed against his chest, and he could not stop his hand from roving up her waist, underneath her shirt.

He expected to feel silk, satin, or some type of restraining cotton but he felt none of those things. Instead, all he felt was the soft expanse of chilled skin and hardened nipples.

Before he could push further, Cate pushed him away with a force of her own.

"No. Not... not yet... We need... I need..." Her words came quickly, as if she were trying to remember how to speak. "There are steps we need to take for this to work." She took a deep breath, and Gunner started to feel the energy within him subsiding, leaving way for sanity to take the driver's seat once more.

"What the hell did you do to me?" he asked as his bearings kicked in.

"Me?" She flashed a look of surprise at him.

"You did something to me."

"Says the man who kissed *me.*"

"You cast some kind of spell on me,

didn't you? That's what this is really about! Thought you'd drag me back here and—"

"Oh, for Heaven's sake, I did nothing."

"That certainly didn't feel like nothing, sweet cheeks."

"Besides, I wouldn't need to cast a spell if all I wanted to do was..." Her voice faded into the night, the words left unsaid aloud.

Cate entered the house once more, leaving Gunner on her doorstep, and this time he did not follow her. Instead, he looked to the full moon above, his wolf pining once more for the magic, the feel of *her*.

Fucking hell.

CHAPTER TWELVE

CATE BRACED HER hands on the countertop and took a deep breath. The chilled feel of the stone felt quite noticeable against her warm palms. Every part of her body felt flush, warm— and she could not deny the wet warmth between her legs, either.

It was just a kiss, for Heaven's sake.

Even as she chastised herself, she could still feel where Gunner had touched her on her skin, where his fingers brushed her nipples.

You're just starved for contact, that's all.

It has nothing to do with him...

She could feel Belle stalking between her feet with admonishment, as if she could read Cate's thoughts.

"Now is not the time, Belladonna." She sighed as Belle meowed at her in judgment.

It had been too long since she'd done a ritual such as this, and the realization struck her that perhaps she was...rusty. Perhaps, she'd jumped in to solve Gunner's shifting problem too quickly.

It wasn't like her to not think through things.

After all, a goddess with much more resolve, much more control, would not spread her legs at the first man that walked through her door after a long dry spell—a century, to be exact.

But there was something about Gunner she could not quite put her finger on, something more than physical.

Something that felt...different.

Yes, he aggravated her, pushed all the buttons that would easily rile her, but yet when he *kissed her...*

There was no rage, no war to win. No stance to be made.

There was only the feeling of absolute *bliss*, of belonging.

Darcy is right. I need to get out more.

Cate returned to her cabinets, grabbing herbs, plants, and tiny rock chips. Her hands shook with tremors and she nearly dropped the vial she needed to fill. She glanced at the grandfather clock in the living room. Three o'clock in the morning. They had but merely three hours until dawn, to pull this off.

Now is not the time to get cold feet, Cate.

With her arms full of supplies, she exited to the backyard once more. Gunner stood in the light of the moon, illuminated like some divine being by its precious light, his dark locks almost silver amongst its glow, the shadows rippling against his defined back muscles. It was then she noticed he had lost his shirt completely. She swallowed as she approached him with more confidence than she felt at the moment.

"I'm going to be honest with you, this may or may not work. It is, quite frankly, not something I've done in over a century, but..."

She stood as tall as she could as she looked up at him.

"Given my power, and your..." She reached her fingers into his hand, feeling the warmth of the moonstone against her own palm. Gunner's fingers held onto hers tightly, and he lightly stroked the inside of her palm with his thumb, an action that elicited tiny shivers down her spine. "Diviner..."

"You don't think it's going to work," he said plainly.

Cate saw a glimmer of hope in his eyes, despite his words. She did not break his gaze.

Suddenly, she felt more than nervous, because she knew what the ritual asked. It was easy to pretend it would be nothing, when she was in the confines of her cabin, but as she looked into Gunner's eyes... it was as if he could see into her very soul, in a way no one was ever truly able to do. Even in all her years of existence, she'd never felt so bare, so exposed to anyone. For the ritual to work, they'd need to connect on both the physical and the spiritual levels, and if his kiss was any indication of how things would go...

She feared she was walking a line she would be far too tempted to cross. A line that would bring her nothing but sorrow, nothing but pain.

For once she served her purpose… once they consummated the ritual, once Cate channeled the manifestation from their sexual bond—

He would not need her.

He would leave, just as all the others had.

She was nothing more than a stepping stone for them—the shifters who'd needed her help, the gods who had also left her bed dry in the wake of their own rewards and goals.

Fame, glory, the spoils of war and victory. She'd given such things to the men who'd promised to give her more.

And they never delivered on their promises. They'd all used her for her power, her magic.

She could not fall victim to such things again.

I know better now; this time it will be different.

"On the contrary, Gunner. I *know* it will work."

She broke his gaze as she knelt down in the dirt and started to draw the proper sigils. She could feel his eyes upon her, his energy in the air. This close, she could feel it heating her skin.

"Then what are you afraid of?" His voice was inquisitive.

She turned to look at him once more, taking in the sight of his perfect features.

He'll make a fine Alpha.

"I fear nothing but the approaching

dawn," she said as the moonlight flared her magic once more. "I will need to go get into something a bit more… comfortable." She cleared her throat as Gunner stood perfectly straight and still, waiting for her to continue. He stood in the center of a large salt circle, lavender, rose, and dried lilies sprinkled throughout salt and black ash.

"You will need to be naked when I return," she said poignantly.

"I beg your pardon?" Gunner snickered, raising an eyebrow.

"For the ritual to work, there will need to be intimate contact."

A sly grin spread on his face.

"Sweet cheeks, if you wanted to see me in my birthday suit…" He slowly started working at the buckle of his belt, and Cate could feel her cheeks flush. "All you had to do was ask." His grin was quite lascivious, and Cate refused to look down as he set to unfastening his belt. He worked at the buttons, sliding his jeans down slowly, never breaking eye contact. Despite wanting to look, she could not bring herself to do so, to give him the satisfaction. She would not give in so easily.

No he will not *enjoy this.*

This is purely not...

"I will return," she said abruptly as she turned on her heel and entered the cabin once more, feeling quite flush.

Spike lifted his head as she walked past, whining for attention as always.

"Not you, too," she groaned as she headed into her bedroom.

There was no reason for her to feel so nervous.

It was just sex magick. She'd practiced it a hundred, a thousand times over her long life.

But it had been a while…

At least, with another person.

Cate rummaged through her wardrobe, in search of something in the right color. Something dark, perhaps something sheer…

Something that would entice an animal out of its cage.

Finally, she settled on a black robe, long and opaque. Simple and understated with velvet trim, tiny silver stars, and moons embroidered into the trim. She lay the robe out on her bed, which was covered in plum velvet comforters and silver throw pillows. Belle meowed from the doorway, judgmental as always.

Cate shut the door, staring at the robe once more before she finally took her shirt off over her head. Her nipples hardened instantly from the chill in the air, and she shivered for a moment as she slid out of her skirt, sliding her panties down. She carefully folded the undergarments, her clothing, and set them out neatly on top of her comforter.

She padded around her bedroom in search of the proper stones she'd need to help channel her power directly. When she finally found her snowflake onyx amulet, she did not think twice about putting it on. One by one, she slid on her rings, her anklet, her long, heavy gemstone chains. Looking in the mirror, she couldn't help but remember a time when such a sight was more than rare, it was *prayed* for.

How men, even gods threw themselves at her feet for just a look.

Let alone a kiss or a fuck.

But the years forced Cate far from the pleasures of flesh, of mortals.

No, *men* had pushed her away, formed her into the solitary statue, the person she was now.

The crazy woman who lives on the edge of the woods.

The weird cat lady who owns the rescue in town.

But as she looked in the mirror, she did not see those things.

Instead, she saw the woman she

thought she had lost.

CHAPTER THIRTEEN

THE EVENING CERTAINLY had not gone as Gunner planned, but in a way it had gone just as Cody wished it would for him.

Go to the speed date thing. Meet a girl. Get laid.

Although the get laid part hadn't

happened, yet…

And it might not if you don't keep your shit together and quit pissing the woman off.

Gunner felt more than exposed standing in the moonlight, naked and waiting. Even now, he could feel his caged wolf pacing inside of him in a way it never had before. Though Cate didn't look like a millennia-old deity. In fact, she looked no older than someone in her late twenties. He could not deny the way his wolf responded to her magic, her presence in the moonlight. He'd tried *everything* else.

Perhaps this is just some twisted joke.

But before he could finish the thought, the sound of the door shutting broke his thoughts.

ARIEL DAWN

His throat was suddenly dry as his gaze settled on the five foot, four inch goddess, whose comfortable clothing consisted of nothing more than a black robe so opaque it left little to the imagination. Her long raven hair tumbled over her shoulders, the one stark silver streak standing out against the darkness like a beam of moonlight.

Black and grey gems adorned her neck, falling to her abdomen, drawing attention to her navel. Her dual-toned eyes glowed of their own accord as she took small barefoot steps toward him. The robe looked to be trimmed in a soft black fabric and boasted silver embroidery that sparkled like diamonds in the light.

She looked positively *breathtaking,*

and his wolf was more than enticed.

He was salivating, waiting for her.

Her touch, her magic.

To feel her, be inside her.

When she stood in front of him, it took all his concentration to remain controlled. He forced himself to focus on her beautiful eyes, eyes that he felt could see into his very soul.

"You look nice," he smirked.

Cate *blushed.*

"It is proper for a ceremony such as this—"

His lips found hers, and he kissed her softly, wistfully, if only for a moment before pulling away.

"You don't take compliments well, do you?" he whispered to her, stealing a glance at her dual-toned eyes once more.

They really were quite stunning.

"I... No. Not anymore." She set her small hand on his chest, her fingers cautiously tracing lines across his skin, the motion leaving a small barrier between them. Space.

Perhaps she doesn't want to do this...

Gunner's wolf panicked.

She doesn't want us.

We have failed again...for the last time.

"We don't have to do this if you don't want to. I mean... I'll be fine, I—"

Cate leaned into him, closing the distance between them with her lips upon his, the movement startling him.

Her kiss was not polite, either, as she snaked her fingers up his chest, along his neck, into his hair, tugging at his locks. She parted her lips, her tongue sliding into his mouth with invitation. Gunner settled his hands against the soft fabric, rustling it as he tried to find the opening. He needed to feel *her*, not some costume.

Her skin, her warmth.

"Gods, why am I like this?" she whispered against his lips, her breath heavy. "Why do you make me like this? I—"

Gunner did not let her finish as he kissed her once more, finding the opening in the center of her robe and shoving it aside. His lips traced her jawline, down to her collarbone, and she let out a sigh of contentment as his fingers traced the skin of her abdomen slowly.

She was softer than he'd expected.

Shifting energy thrummed in his veins, and his wolf rose to the surface, but it didn't hurt. Not this time.

It was a maddening feeling, the need.

Like he'd never have enough.

Cate's words came out in hurried, breathy whispers.

Words Gunner could not quite comprehend because they were in a language he'd never heard before. He continued to push at her robe, slide his hands across her abdomen. His fingers brushed above the small of her back, across her ass. Down her thighs…

The words she chanted somehow incensed him more as he slid her robe off her shoulders, making haste of his movement.

There needs to be nothing between us...

He felt everything, but it was as if *he* was not the only one who could feel.

Who could want.

His wolf wanted more, wanted to feel what he could.

He longed to be free.

Cate pushed him away for a moment, and the unfamiliar words stopped.

"Gunner..." she breathed his name heavily, and the sound of it, of his name on her tongue like that...

His cock throbbed against her.

"Do..." Gunner tried to catch his breath, his head spinning from the maddening thoughts and feelings running through him. "Do you want me to stop?" he asked.

"No, I... I need to dress you first." She cleared her throat.

"What's wrong, sweet cheeks? This body too much for you already?" he teased.

Cate narrowed her eyes at him, and her annoyance showed.

"I can assure you, once this ritual commences, I will be too much for your mortal body to handle. Your wolf will have to take over." She smiled devilishly.

"Is that so?" He reached out and brushed her silver hair over her shoulder with a smirk.

"I need to anoint you in the proper oils, and say a spell first. Then..." Cate paused as if struggling to find the right words.

"What's the matter? Cat got your

tongue?" Gunner drawled.

"We will need to consummate the ritual. Manifest the energy built between our bodies, and..."

"You are nervous."

"I am not..." Cate huffed.

"When you're nervous, you start talking clinically. Your eyes do this little back and forth thing." Gunner reached out a hand to her hip, pulling her body close, and he did not miss how she relaxed at his touch. How she leaned into him, her breasts brushing against his chest softly, though she did not meet his gaze.

"Cate..." His voice turned serious. "What you're doing for me, this ritual... it doesn't have to be one-sided, you know." With his free hand, he ran his fingers through her luscious silken locks. His gaze roved over her form, finally settling on her perfect lips. Lips he wanted to kiss again and again.

He'd never felt this way about anyone, and though he knew such things should be alarming, he had to admit he felt no danger.

Cate traced her fingers along the back of his hand. "Yes, it does. I can't..."

"Can't what?" He brushed his fingers over her cheek.

Cate looked up at him, her fingers finding their way up his neck, tracing lines down his jaw. Lightly brushing across his lips.

Her eyes sparkled, and the way she looked at him... A startling feeling built inside of his chest, one he'd never felt in all his thirty-one years. His heartbeat quickened from the realization of what it was he felt.

Love.

It was crazy to think a woman he'd just met could have this effect on him.

A woman who the Diviner had recognized.

A woman who was somehow meant for him.

His mate.

The spirit inside of him longed to soothe her, to make her feel cherished, loved.

Worshipped.

It was a most surprising feeling.

Gunner had never been in love. Not the true kind, the kind sanctioned by the Diviner, the kind where he and his wolf knew it belonged to a mate.

Not like this.

Cate stared back at him as if she contemplated her words very carefully. In her eyes, he could see the pain, her struggle.

What asshole is responsible for that? He wondered.

"Sit down, Gunner," she said solidly.

The moment of vulnerability had passed, and suddenly everything was different.

Instead of bristling against the command or irking her with a sarcastic response, Gunner simply obeyed as he sat against the tree on the soft earth, surrounded by a circle of salt, herbs, flowers, and sigils. He looked up at the goddess and awaited her instruction once more.   174

CHAPTER FOURTEEN

CATE'S ENTIRE BODY felt warm from the slightest touch of Gunner's fingers on her skin.

As if…

As if something inside her that lay dormant had also been awakened.

Something she had forgotten long

ago.

Cate gazed upon the fine specimen in her backyard as she gently knelt down to her discarded robe to retrieve her ceremonial oil vial. She approached him, putting herself directly in the moonlight's path, and her entire body felt alive with sparks, with magic that knew it was needed.

Alive with purpose.

She stepped one foot into the circle, then the other.

Gunner looked up at her with dark, mysterious eyes, and in them she could see he was nervous, too.

Cate suspected Gunner feared the ritual would not work because he'd accepted his fate as a failed shifter.

The anguish that acceptance brought,

the never-ending internal fight he must have had to endure...

Cate felt a stirring in her being at that knowledge.

Sadness.

She wanted to free his spirit, but it had been far too long since she'd engaged in *sex magick*, manifestations, and rituals such as this. Despite her concerns, her own inclinations, something about Gunner pulled at her, begged her to listen, to hear it.

Diviner or no Diviner, she had already strayed too far into the process, and there was truly no turning back now.

There was no way out, except through, and Cate only hoped she would make it out unscathed.

"Lie down," she instructed him. "Arms out, like a cross." She watched as the naked Gunner slid down onto the cool earth, as he spread his arms out like branches. She took in the sight of him, sprawled on the moist earth; the curve of his biceps, the definition of his form, the rather pleasing cut of his hip bones. Shadows fell across his skin, and he looked positively stunning against the darkness of the night.

She knelt beside him softly and poured the oil on his chest, down his abdomen in one, long steady stream.

He did not even flinch.

She took a deep breath before chanting the ancient words that came to her so easily now, like riding a bicycle.

Here goes nothing...

Cate slowly crawled over Gunner, straddling him as she closed her eyes.

She could feel the pull of the magic from the earth below, the shifting energy beneath the surface of his body, and her own sparks igniting in the beam of light that cast down upon them.

It was like hearing one solid voice in a crowded room, and it beckoned her to fall into the abyss.

She repeated the words, trying to focus on them, but all concentration was lost when she felt the twitching of Gunner's cock against her entrance.

Focus, Cate!

She opened her eyes to see Gunner staring at her.

"You don't have to close your eyes." His voice was steady, and he looked at her as if…

As if she were the sun, the moon, and the stars.

The feeling was most… *moving.*

"It is easier to manage my concentration if I do not have to look at you."

"I know the feeling," he whispered. "It's hard for me to concentrate when my wolf is pushing against my ribcage because a hot naked goddess is about to fuck the animal right out of me."

Cate could not help the smile that spread on her lips.

The fire in this one…

"Ah, so you do have a sense of humor," he purred, and Cate could not help the small laugh that escaped her. But then all laughter dissipated in the midnight air, his breath the only sound between them once more.

Gunner slid his hand up her thigh slowly, and she felt a maddening blush once more as his thumb grazed her entrance only slightly.

"I meant what I said, Cate. This doesn't have to be something solely for my benefit." His free hand cupped her ass, and she couldn't deny the feeling sent a jolt of electricity right through her.

"Gunner..." she groaned both in defiance and in desperation.

"How long has it been?" he asked as his fingers traced lines along her ass.

"I beg your pardon?" She swallowed, her mouth suddenly dry.

"How long has it been since anyone

gave you an orgasm?"

Cate froze.

She wasn't entirely sure how to answer his question.

It had been centuries since she'd lain with a mortal man, centuries since she'd engaged in the ritual to set a caged spirit free.

Even the one night stands she'd engaged in—Thor, Lucifer, that one priest from Budapest...

No man had ever really pleased her in the way Gunner was insinuating.

Gunner must have taken her silence for an answer, and she cursed herself for being so transparent.

"Come here," he commanded, his voice dark and inviting.

"What?" Cate said, still frozen in

place.

Gunner gently tugged at her hips, the motion dragging her forward, up his body, away from his groin. "I said, come here." He growled as he pulled her forward with more force this time, setting her just above his throat.

She thought for a moment she could surely kill him in such a position.

Squeeze her thighs around his neck, stop him from breathing.

It would be much easier, but the sight of him beneath her ignited something else, some long forgotten desire, some long forgotten feeling. A feeling she'd missed, in all honesty. She shifted her hips forward without a second thought, and in return she was met with a wet, warm tongue, which licked at all the right places, causing sparks to dance along her skin once more. The moist feel of his tongue as it lapped around her clit, as it caressed her outer folds, finding its way inside her, caused her thighs to tighten and forced her to cry out without warning.

Her breath shuddered and the power inside forced her way to the surface once more as Cate bucked her hips forward, forcing his tongue deeper. Each thrust forward against his torturous mouth shattered something within her, walls she'd kept up far too long.

Gunner's caged wolf, it seemed, had awakened a monster within her as well, and she was so very *hungry*.

Cate's insides twisted, and a maddening build started to form, the hunger spreading throughout her body like fire catching in a dead, dry forest. The moan that escaped her throat felt full and raw, and not something Cate could control.

She had to admit, she didn't want to control it.

She wanted more of it.

More of Gunner's hot mouth, more of the feeling of satisfaction building within.

Gunner's hands squeezed at the flesh of her ass as he slid one finger in, probing her gently, and she could not hold her ecstasy in any longer.

CHAPTER FIFTEEN

GUNNER'S WOLF SURGED against its cage once more, and for a moment the spirit danced above the waves of his desire.

The golden-green glow hovered inches above him, struggling, straining, as if despite all its strength something still tethered it to the ground.

As soon as it had breached, it was pulled back under, for Cate's cries of pleasure broke through the silent air.

His gaze traveled upward, taking in the sight of her like this.

Long, dark hair falling wildly around her shoulders covering her breasts in haphazard strands, pale skin illuminated in the moonlight, dancing with sparks. Perfect, taut pink nipples standing out against the creamy expanse of her porcelain skin.

Eyes shut tight, chest heaving as she rode the waves of her release.

His cock throbbed with anticipation as Cate rolled off of him and onto the ground beside him, refusing to look at him. She lay by his side, her hand on her heart, eyes staring straight up at the moon.

Gunner pulled himself up to his elbows and glanced over at her, a strange silence befalling them.

"Well, that should take the edge off." He chuckled.

"It wasn't enough." She spoke solidly but did not look at him.

Excuse me?

"You think I'm done with you?" He rolled over onto his side, slinking closer to her.

Cate cast him a look that told him to stay where he lay. Not to push further.

"This is not about me." She swallowed as she rolled over onto her side, little bits of earth sticking to her pale skin. The sight enticed his wolf, and images of

Cate being driven into the soil forced their way into his brain. He cleared his throat, if only to push them aside for the moment.

"This is about you." She pulled herself closer, setting her hand on his chest. Tiny zaps of magic danced on his skin. "Stand up. I have an idea," she directed him.

Gunner, feeling only marginally slighted after his display, did as he was told, and she stood in tandem. Cate's dual-toned gaze roved over his body, and he did not miss the glow in her eyes.

Or the hunger in them.

Something tried to be released within her as well, it seemed. She angled herself closer, bringing her warm body flush against his, and his cock twitched. He longed for release, unsure of how long he would be able to stand the anticipation. She set her hand on his chest once again, but this time it was not gentle. Her nails bit into his oil-slicked chest, and she pushed him hard against the tree.

When she brought her lips to his, they were full of fire, full of need.

Sparks danced along her skin like fractals, blue and green, and a gentle wind chilled him, blowing her hair around them.

Gunner could not help the groan that escaped his mouth, or the rattle of his wolf pushing forth.

A deep growl sounded from his chest, like the rumble of thunder.

Cate reached down, clasping her

fingers around his aching cock. Her tongue forced its way into his mouth, eliciting another deep, satisfied groan.

The energy pulsed above his skin, hovering only slightly.

"More," he moaned into her mouth.

Cate's fingernails bit into the skin of his chest. "You do not tell me what to do. Do you understand?" she growled in response.

Gunner's lips twitched in a smile.

"Or what, sweet cheeks? You're going to bend me over your knee and punish me?" he teased.

"Perhaps a good punishment is just what you need to root out that defiance."

Her lips brushed the skin of his neck, trailing saliva down his shoulder as she stopped at his pectoral, taking a solid nipple into her mouth.

The feeling was rather nice...

Until she bit down on him.

"Fuck!" Gunner yelled in surprise.

Her lips turned up a smile as she gazed up at him, glowing dual eyes be damned.

"Now, if you don't mind, I'd like to do my work," she breathed huskily, and Gunner throbbed in her hand as she squeezed him tightly.

He nodded, a silent response.

She whispered ancient words, and he had to admit they sounded quite beautiful on her tongue. The wind picked up, rustling the trees, and the earth upon which he stood felt flush and warm, like a blanket of fire. His head started to feel quite hazy, and his wolf surged forth, hungry for the magic that called to it.

For her.

Her lips torturously wandered across his chest, her tongue licking in the grooves of his muscle, drawing wet lines of desire down to his aching cock.

He could feel the tiniest drop of wetness emerge, and his head fell back against the tree with a thud. No sooner had his eyes closed did he feel the warmth of her tongue along the underside of his shaft, and the shock of the feeling caused a growl to escape.

It wasn't a human growl. This was something much deeper, much darker.

Much more primal.

When Cate slid all of him into her mouth, he couldn't help his own cries of passion.

"Fuck..." he said, his voice cracking.

He'd had plenty of blowjobs in his thirty-one years of life, especially due to the fact he was built like a brick house and a supposed heir to the Brickman line, but no one's mouth had ever felt *this* good around his cock.

The familiar tightening in his balls started to form, and Gunner started to panic.

"Not yet," he cried.

Cate did not seem to hear him.

"Cate..." He tried to find the words, to tell her to stop. "Cate... I'm..."

The pleasure hit him, and the energy pulled him forward, lurching deeper into the back of her throat. The motion was too much, and he could not stop as she rolled her tongue around him, coaxing out his release. His eyes strained shut, and he could not help as he grabbed her by the hair, spilling himself into her with a release that caused him to see stars behind his eyes.

"Fuck." He repeated the words as his high started to break.

Cate slowly dislodged him from her mouth, swallowing his ecstasy.

Gunner slid down against the tree, the warm earth seeping up around him once more as he deigned to catch his breath.

Cate smiled proudly.

"What the fuck are you smiling about?" he grumbled.

"I told you I would be too much for your mortal body to handle. You did not believe me."

She slowly sat down next to him, placing a hand on his thigh.

Gunner took a deep breath.

"Well, I'm spent now. So, I guess your little sexcapade didn't work." He sighed.

"Who says I'm done with you?" she touted back to him.

He opened his eyes and raised a brow at her. "I'm going to need a minute." He couldn't help the laugh in his voice.

"No, you don't. You just need to engage your wolf. Trust me, he'll have no problem bringing you up to speed." She let out a small chuckle, and despite the situation, Gunner had to admit he felt...

At ease.

Happy.

"Right. Well, if I knew how to *engage*

my wolf, I wouldn't be here."

Cate scooted closer to him, close enough her silky hair fell on his shoulder. He stole a glance downward at her, taking in the sight of her beauty once more.

Mate.

His heart skipped a beat.

How have I lived my entire life without her?

How did I not know she existed?

The feelings, the thoughts were foreign to him, but he embraced them.

For in her presence, it was hard to ignore them all.

"You need only give in to the desires and the wants of your wolf. Hear his pleas. You must want to let him take over. Give him permission to do so."

"If it was only that simple." He closed his eyes once more.

"It is that simple. You have to let go of what is holding you back."

"Nothing is holding me back," he whispered.

Small hands touched his face gently, pulling him away from his thoughts.

"You do not have to lie to me. I know what it is like to feel out of control. To feel like losing it means losing yourself." Her nails traced his jaw, and her eyes fixated on his lips.

"You will not hurt me. You are in no danger here."

Her words somehow stirred the wolf within, and he was not full of rage or lust.

But instead, he pined.

The surge forth was not painful, not shocking.

It felt *good.*

To be understood.

To be wanted.

And when Gunner looked into Cate's glowing eyes, he understood for the first time that perhaps he and his wolf wanted the same thing.

CHAPTER SIXTEEN

GUNNER LOOKED AT Cate, the shifter glow vivid in his amber eyes, turning them to gold. She'd expected to see so many things this far into the ritual.

Hunger.

Need.

Lust.

But what she saw instead caused her stomach to flip.

Gunner looked at her like she was *his.*

Her heart lurched in her chest, and she had to fight the surge of emotion within her at the sight.

Gunner closed the space between him with the softest kiss.

It wasn't a kiss of fire, or ice.

It wasn't something purely for sexual gain, either.

Instead, it was the kind of kiss that destroyed empires. The kind of kiss that got scribbled on papyrus or on ancient walls, the kind that playwrights and musicians wrote about.

A kiss of absolute love.

Cate knew as she kissed Gunner,

tasted the remnants of herself on his tongue, that if all the time they had was this fleeting moment, she would savor what she could.

Because she knew in the thousands of years she'd lived, and the thousands she would live thereafter, no one would ever kiss her like this. Not again.

Her magic prickled against her skin, this time much more vibrant, and Gunner's wolf responded in tune. They sat there in the marked dirt, glowing tendrils of blue and green and yellow dancing like ribbons around them, bathed in the light of the full moon.

Dawn would be approaching before too long.

The night would cease, and with it Gunner would go.

To his home, his family.

To his life.

The life he'd been living before she stumbled upon him, drunk in a bar at a speed dating event.

"Give him permission, Gunner. Let go," she whispered the words against his lips, and though she spoke the truth, somehow the words were something else in her brain.

What she'd longed to say was, "Don't go. Stay."

Gunner shifted his body forward, his large arms circling her waist, fingers splayed at her back as he pulled her close once more. The touch was firm and wanting, and Cate wanted to melt into a puddle.

Which was *insane.*

No woman or man had ever managed to breach her defenses quite like this, let alone so quickly, but Cate could not deny it felt right.

Her eyes caught a bright, blinding light sparkling not far from where they sat twisted together. The low hum of magic buzzing in her ears felt most noticeable to her, although she was certain Gunner could not hear it. Though he was a shifter, he was still mortal. Her kind created it, after all.

The Diviner sang its whistling tune, and the power beneath the earth hummed along with it. In the moonlight her own magic echoed with the symphony around them, joined by the vibrations of a caged spirit that longed to be part of the band. As her eyes fixed on the glowing moonstone, the conductor in this magical orchestra, she understood completely why she felt this way.

Because the Diviner did not lie.

It told the truth.

It showed you your mate.

Your true love.

The notion saddened Cate. Love was something she had truly given up on. After years of watching wars and battles over it, after watching civilizations crumble in the wake of it, she'd garnered that love was not the splendid thing humans thought it was.

It was a dangerous weapon, and in the hands of the wrong—where it often ended up—it was rather deadly.

She'd watched Hades and Persephone fall so madly in love that they nearly discarded everything. She'd watched him obsess, pine, and fight against his feelings, only to give in. When she'd seen him in the middle of the night, stealing Persephone from her home, she'd assumed the worst; that he'd gone mad and stepped out of line. She had not quite understood at the time what had transpired, and when Demeter came to her for help, she'd obliged, if only for the fact she could talk some sense into her friend. When she'd discovered Persephone had left of her own accord, given up everything to be with Hades; ignorant to the turmoil and repercussions of that decision... Cate understood in that moment love was not a bright and beautiful thing.

It was a blinding, all-consuming thing

that seduced you with its illusions of grandeur.

And in the end she'd left, too.

After being the be-all and end-all of Hades' entire existence, she'd *forgotten* him. Her memory of him had been completely erased, and she'd forged a new life, leaving her true love to wither in the darkness without the blink of an eye.

It had taken Hades ages to piece himself back together.

Hades had told her that life was to be lived in the moment. She'd never truly understood his sentiment, being one who serviced the dead and all, but at this moment she finally felt as if she understood what he meant.

That the joys of life were as rare and

fleeting as a blue moon. They came and went in a flash, and if you were not careful, you'd miss them.

Cate found herself in the presence of glowing golden eyes, and when her lips crashed against Gunner's, she gave into the temptation.

Because if all they had was this moment, she did not want to waste it.

CHAPTER SEVENTEEN

CATE PULLED GUNNER closer, and he followed her without question.

A deep sigh left Gunner's throat, and he pushed her down into the dirt.

Earth's energy surged beneath her, warming her chilled skin.

Gunner's shoulders tensed as the

weight of his body slid over top of her.

Cate traced her fingers up his jaw, feeling the prickly stubble, the feel of his skin against her fingertips.

His lips broke away from hers, and the sight of his golden eyes called to the power within, igniting her. She could feel the magic all around her, and even if she couldn't feel it, she'd know. For she could see the reflection of her opalescent glowing eyes in his.

Her hands traveled down his chest, nails digging into his skin, feeling the slick oil mixed with hard muscle.

Her head started to spin.

Gunner grabbed her wrists, a deep growl escaping him as he pushed them down beside her. There was something in the way he touched her, the way he held her wrists...

She did not fight.

His lips found their way to her neck, and he bit at her taut skin. Razor sharp fangs drawing faint lines along the vein in her neck.

His cock throbbed against her, and she longed to move her legs from beneath him, to wrap them around his waist like a vice.

Fangs.

Gunner's wolf has surfaced.

Finally, it's working.

The transition is starting.

His fingernails bit into her skin as he held her with a force she could only describe as primal. Gunner ran his tongue down her collarbone, trailing hot kisses along her skin. When he stopped for a moment, Cate wanted to protest, but she was not given the chance. When Gunner took her nipple between his fangs, resistance was futile.

He released her wrists, one hand squeezing her breast tightly as he licked and sucked, the other sliding down her hips, fingers tracing lines of dirt along her thigh.

With her hands free, she abruptly fixed them in his hair, tugging at the locks.

The sound of her soft moan elicited another deep rumble from his throat.

Gunner drew his lips up from their current fascination, and he looked at her with fire in his golden eyes, lips pulled back showcasing his long, bright white fangs.

A warm, satisfying wetness blossomed between Cate's legs at the sight, and she could not help the words that came out of her mouth.

"Take me. Now." She breathed deep as she said the words, her body hot like fire.

"Turn over," he growled.

Cate raised her eyebrows at the sound, for it was far too commanding and direct to be anything but the tone of an Alpha wolf.

Cate did not like to be told what to do, nor did she like to obey anyone.

She was a goddess for fuck's sake.

She smiled haughtily. "Make me."

"My pleasure," he growled as he grabbed her abruptly, fingers digging into her skin. His grip was welcome, but also quite surprising when he twisted her, flipping her around like she was nothing more than a rag doll. Gunner's voice was smooth and sexy, but in those two words she heard a darkness, a desire within it that told her he was close to the edge, close to being freed.

His right hand held her at her waist, pulling her back to him. His free hand gripped her ass, stroking it with his palm smoothly, running his fingers up her spine until he reached her neck. Gunner pushed her down with one hand, while the other, which held her at her waist, traveled below her navel down to her entrance, fingertips stroking her wet folds.

Instinctually, Cate arched her back, pushing back against him.

"Don't move," he ordered, and she held her breath, knowing what was coming. She nodded in compliance.

He removed his hand from her neck and lined himself up.

The moment of waiting lasted an eternity. But when Gunner pushed himself inside her, Cate felt as if eternity would never be long enough.

His thrusts were hard and fast, and they stirred something primal within her, called to her magic like a reckoning.

Gunner's hand found her hair once more, fingers twisting in her silken locks.

The scent of sacred oils, of sweat, and arousal perfumed the air, clouding her airways.

The rhythmic drag and force flamed

the building inferno within Cate, until she could not hold back her own desires anymore.

When Gunner slid out of her, she scrambled to her feet and turned around, shoving him into the dirt, her hand on his chest, magic erupting from her fingertips.

Gunner growled darkly in response, and moved to stand, but he was not successful.

Cate did not give him the chance as she straddled him once more, sliding on to him, thighs trapping him beneath her. She braced her hands against his wrists, and a growl escaped her throat as, fangs of her own pushing through.

Gunner's eyes widened in surprise, but the name on his tongue drove her over the edge.

"Hecate," he whispered in awe.

CHAPTER EIGHTEEN

GUNNER GAZED UP at the goddess before him. Her natural two-toned eyes had gone full white. The magic that shimmered along her skin was no longer fractals, but rather as if it were *within* her. Her pale skin glowed like moonstone, her dark hair rustling in the gentle breeze that surrounded her. She bared her fangs at him, and Gunner thought for sure this was how it all ended.

And if it was the end, it was not a terrible way to go.

Gunner felt trapped beneath the surface of his own body as his wolf separated itself, coming to the surface fully.

Taking over, and for once he was glad to let his wolf drive the car.

Because he was quite certain Cate... no, *Hecate*... was right.

His mortal body would not be able to handle her.

Because just the sight of her as she rode his dick, taking her own pleasure from him, made him want to explode into a million pieces, nevermind how it felt to be inside her warm, slick walls.

Better than anything I've ever felt in my entire damn life.

She let go of his wrists, and he did not waste the chance to touch her, feel her, grab her. He needed every bit of her he could have, and somehow every bit would not be enough.

He'd *never* get enough of this woman.

His mate.

Gunner sank his fingernails into the flesh of her juicy ass as he thrust up into her.

It was all quite a maddening blur; rushed hands, and lips on lips, kissing, biting...

Gunner sat up, wrapping his arms around Cate's body, lips seeking out breasts and nipples, fingers stroking her entrance, her clit, as he filled her. Her fangs bit down on his shoulder as her walls fluttered around his cock, and the sound of her release... He could not hold his own release back at the sound as he emptied himself into her with a final deep thrust, severing all the remaining tethers, like one cuts the string of a balloon.

Everything was somehow sharper, more pronounced, and he could have sworn he heard a sob.

Is she crying?

But before he could soothe his mate, an earthquake rumbled beneath them.

No, *inside* of him.

Cate dislodged herself from him, and he hated how empty he felt afterward.

That distaste soon gave way to something much more intense.

Pain.

Gunner's bones snapped and popped, and the feeling was awful.

As if he were dying.

He tried to speak, to say anything, but words would not come out of his mouth, only growls and grunts that sounded more animal than human.

His muscles reformed around the shape of new bones, and his back arched. His spine tingled with a numbing sensation as he doubled over onto the ground, fingers digging into the earth to hold on.

Claws forced their way through the edges of his fingertips, and the world blurred once more. Gunner shut his eyes to keep the dizziness at bay, and when he opened them again, he could not believe what he saw.

Paws.

Large, white paws.

Sounds of the forest were sharp, his eyesight so much clearer than before, and one startling realization took over everything.

I am a wolf.

I have finally shifted.

Instinctually, he knew what to do. He'd been waiting his whole life for this moment.

So Gunner lifted his head to the moon, and he howled.

The echoes of wolves in the distance answered his call, and Gunner felt complete.

CHAPTER NINETEEN

CATE TOOK IN the sight of the beautiful wolf before her, and though she was happy Gunner had finally shifted, her heart broke knowing this was the last she'd ever see of him.

The tears rolled down her face without warning, and a sob escaped. She wiped a tear away quickly as she watched Gunner throw his head back and howl. When the answer of his kind sounded in the night, she knew it would not be long.

The white wolf's eyes turned toward her, amber rimmed in beautiful gold.

"Go. Be with your pack." She forced a smile.

Gunner cocked his head to the side.

"My work here is done. Your wolf is free. You are both free."

Gunner approached her swiftly, nuzzling his head against her bare legs. Cate sobbed again as she let her fingers stroke his soft fur.

"Goodbye, Gunner," she said through tears.

The wolf whined, and she turned

away, taking up residence in her cabin once more, locking the door. Cate slid down the door, and in the walls of her home she let go completely. She wrapped her arms around her knees, burying her head in her arms, and she cried, heart-wracking sobs.

Spike padded over to her, nuzzling her side as Gunner had, and a whole new surge of guilt and sadness tore through her. She pulled the hellhound to her. Spike whined next to her, setting his paw on her foot. Belle meowed, making her presence known. She wrapped her tail around Cate's calf, brushing her head against her sweetly.

Cate could hear the howls outside and a scratching at her door. How badly she wanted to open the door, let Gunner in. He had a life, a family, a lineage to uphold. She could not take those things away from him, and she wouldn't. Immortality was not designed for mortals.

Mortals with fragile hearts, driven by emotions.

By love.

Love was not meant for creatures, like herself.

She'd watched far too many loves of lifetimes end in despair, and she would not allow herself to feel such things. Not this time.

It will be different this time.

Gunner would live his life as he should. Perhaps now that he had shifted, he'd take over his pack. Find a wife, have some heirs. Die at a ripe old age, as life had intended for him.

And that would have to be enough.

Cate did not realize the scratching had stopped until the sun peeked through her windows. She held onto Spike, a purring Belle at her side, and only then, when she was certain it was over, did she rise from her spot on the floor.

The dawn of a new day was here, and once again, Cate was alone.

But it is better this way, isn't it?

CHAPTER TWENTY

GUNNER'S FATHER RAISED his beer in toast. A celebration was due, as Gunner had finally shifted and was ready to take his spot as Alpha in the Brickman pack. It was his destiny. He had been rallying toward this one, very clear thing since he was a small child.

So why do I feel so empty?

But it was pointless. He knew the answer.

Because she was gone.

His mate.

The Keeper of the Wolves.

Hecate.

Sweet cheeks.

It had been five days.

Five days since he'd listened to Cody, since he'd met Cate. Since the ritual had worked and set his caged spirit free.

Five days since he'd felt the utter bliss of making love to his mate.

Nothing felt right without her.

She'd shut him out, and locked the door. He couldn't understand why.

Did she not feel the mate bond between them as he did?

Surely, she had.

So why does she reject me?

Even as his father made his speech, as he walked around the field in which they'd planned his Succession Party, he thought of her.

He needed to find her.

Gunner wandered around the field by himself, taking in the sight of the forest and the trees. When his gaze settled on a man in a dark suit and a brunette with far too much cheer for a Sunday afternoon, he was about to turn heel. He didn't need to see happy couples.

Not now.

But the man called his name.

"Gunner! Is that you?"

Gunner stopped as the man and woman approached him. He was certain he had never seen this man before, dressed in his fine Italian suit, dark hair and eyes, but something about his voice sounded familiar. The woman with chestnut hair and bright blue eyes looked back at him with curiosity.

He did not know these people; he was sure of it. So how did they know him?

"I'm sorry, I—"

"He doesn't know who we are, H. He was unconscious, remember?" The woman rolled her eyes, her lips pulling up in the corners into a smile.

Who are these people?

"Unconscious…"

"Forgive my manners, yeah… I guess you wouldn't remember us." The man smiled.

"We are friends of Cate's." The woman

nodded as she took in the sight of Gunner.

Gunner's heart stopped.

"You are friends with Cate?" He repeated the words solidly.

The woman nodded. "I'm Darcy, and this here is..." She looked at the man before answering. "H."

"That short for something?" Gunner asked as he took a swig of his beer, wondering if his madness had started to cause delusions.

"Hades." The man Darcy called "H" smiled devilishly.

"Like the—"

"God of the Underworld, yes. We've been over this." Hades rolled his eyes.

"Unconscious, H," Darcy reminded him.

"Do you...." Gunner swallowed quickly. "Do you know where to find her?" he asked, not one to waste chances. The run through the forest, to find his wolves was a blur. His animal propelled him through, driven him into the company of his fellow wolves.

Though Gunner knew he should be able to find Cate's cabin easily, it was as if there was something preventing him from doing so. He'd walked the woods tirelessly in search, but every search came up empty. He'd started to wonder if he'd imagined it all, but he knew he hadn't.

Hades looked at Darcy with worry.

"What do you mean? Surely, you know—"

"I know this is going to sound crazy,

but..." Gunner slid his hand in his jeans pocket, pulling out his Diviner. "This rock—"

"That's the one from the other night!" Darcy plucked the stone clean out of Gunner's hand. He raised his eyebrow in shock.

"Darcy, don't touch that!" Hades made a beeline for the stone, his fingers brushing it in Darcy's palm, and the moonstone glowed once more. No one seemed to pass out from contact, so Gunner supposed that was an improvement.

"The Diviner predicts your mate." Gunner cleared his throat, noting the tendrils that danced between Darcy and Hades. Both looked at him with surprise. "Cate is my mate. She—"

"Say no more." Hades shook his head.

"Really?" Gunner felt a smile course over his lips.

"I have known Cate since what you humans would call the dawn of time," Hades pulled a pen from his suit pocket and a Post-It note pad.

"You keep Post-It notes on you?" Darcy raised her eyebrow at him.

"When I come topside, yes. So I can write down all the things I didn't do. Things I can do next time."

"Can't you use a phone like a normal person?" Darcy asked.

"You imply I am a normal person, Darcy. Surely, you know better by now. I am far from normal."

Gunner stifled a laugh.

"As I was saying before I was *rudely*

interrupted." Hades smirked. "I have known Cate for quite some time. If what you say is true, you will need to do some worshipping. Cate believes no one can love her, mate or not."

Darcy frowned.

"It's the immortality thing," Darcy chimed in.

Hades perked his head up from his Pos-It.

"What?"

"The immortality thing. If you're mated to a god, and you're mortal..." She averted Hades' gaze. "Mortals die. We can't live forever." Darcy's voice seemed to have lost all cheer.

"Death is not always physical." Hades looked at her seriously. "You can be alive, but not *alive*."

Gunner felt as if he was witnessing something he had no business seeing.

"Think about it, H. You know her. She doesn't want to watch him—"

"There are deals that can be made, Darcy. Sometimes, life defies the odds." Hades handed him the Post-It note with not just an address, but instructions.

And a list.

Gunner's eyes caught on the name listed for the address.

Cate Moon.

What a beautiful name.

"You'll only have one shot, so don't waste it." Hades looked at him seriously now.

"Absolutely not."

CHAPTER TWENTY-ONE

CATE GENTLY STROKED the kitten she held in her arms. He'd finally dozed off after his feeding, and she hated to put him down. She patted the soft spot between his ears, feeling the vibrations of his tiny body purring against her chest.

"You should keep him," Darcy said as she placed a cup full of steaming tea in front of Cate.

"Perhaps, I should get another pet." Cate shrugged. "I'm sure Belle and Spike could use the company."

"I saw Gunner at the park today." Darcy's tone was careful, and Cate stopped her pacing.

"What?"

"You didn't tell me about the Diviner—"

"It doesn't matter, Darcy."

"Yes, it does. Cate, I know I haven't know you as long as Hades has—"

Cate pursed her lips at the casual mention of her friend's name. While she was happy Hades had found someone he enjoyed being around since Persephone, she was concerned.

Mortals and gods…

It was such a touchy thing. Sure, they were sexually compatible, but the length of life… unless a deal was brought forth and sanctioned by the right god…

Life was the blink of an eye for a god. A century was a bathroom break. She did not want to watch Hades fall in love only to be broken again.

"Life is lived in moments, right?" Darcy's voice softened.

Cate continued to pace, focusing on her purring machine in her arms. His warmth. "I suppose."

"Then fill those little moments with love. All the little things, the tiny details…" Darcy spoke with a clarity Cate had never heard before. She was usually so aloof, so fickle about such things as love.

The tone moved Cate to listen.

"If all you have is today, Cate... make today your forever. And when you wake up tomorrow, you do the same."

"It isn't that simple, Darcy." Cate could feel the stirrings of hope within her chest, and she dared to give in.

"It is absolutely that simple, Cate. He is your *mate*."

The words on Darcy's tongue were so very clear to Cate, and her heart beat with anticipation.

And as if perfectly on cue, the door to the New Haven Animal Rescue opened, and there he stood. Perfectly illuminated in the fluorescent light, holding a small gathering of black roses.

He smirked a nonchalant, cocky smirk, sliding his hand into his pocket. Amber eyes rimmed in gold once more.

Cate suddenly found it difficult to breathe.

"Cate..."

She didn't wait for him to finish as she strode across the tiled floor and found herself in front of him, drawn to him like an invisible tether.

"You came back..." Her voice was a whisper.

Gunner's lips turned up in a cocky smile as he held up the roses. "And I came with presents."

Cate blushed.

"I didn't think..." She could not find words, and even if she could she would not have spoken any.

Gunner claimed her lips with his, and the wind rustled around the both of them. Stirred by the magic, the bond between them.

When they broke apart, Gunner reached out and ran his hand through her hair.

"You thought what? That you'd just fuck me and leave me? I should be pissed, but if you weren't the best sex I've ever had, sweet cheeks..."

"Does that sort of talk work on all the girls?" she teased.

"Only the goddesses." He smiled.

Cate rolled her eyes.

"You're going to have to do a little better than some ill-fated pick up lines and a bouquet of flowers." She turned away with a sly smile.

"How about dinner? I know this great place—"

"Eight PM. You will meet me here."

"Isn't—"

"You will do as I say," she stated firmly, smiling at Darcy, who looked positively giddy.

"We'll see about that," he answered with a deep growl.

"Yes, I suppose we will."

Thanks for reading!

Follow our Facebook page here: <u>Speed Dating with the Denizens of the Underworld Series</u>

Watch your favorite online retailer for the other books in the Speed Dating with the Denizens of the Underworld series.

Turn the page now for an excerpt from *Bastet by Laura Greenwood*, Book Seven in the Speed Dating with the Denizens of the Underworld series!

EXCERPT

Bastet knows better than to fall for her ex, and yet she can't seem to help herself.

WHY HAD I let myself get talked into this? I hadn't been around this many people in a long time, and there was a good reason for that. I was much more comfortable in a one on one situation.

"Hello, Bastet," a familiar voice said.

I looked up, slightly alarmed despite knowing he was in the room. "Ptah." His name came out as a cracked whisper, one that I hadn't used in a long time.

He pulled his chair out and sat down, his gorgeous dark eyes piercing me and seeing right into my soul.

Ptah had always had something about him that made me feel as if he understood me on a level no one else ever had.

"I didn't expect to see you tonight," he said.

"Surprised I'm dating?"

He chuckled, a throaty sound that reminded me of intimate moments and stolen kisses. "I'm more surprised that I am," he joked. "This is my first time."

"What made you decide to join in?"

A smirk lifted the corner of his lips. "Let's just say there was something that intrigued me about tonight."

The way he studied me made it almost possible to think he was doing all of this because of me. But I doubted that. We hadn't been together for a long time, and we broke up for very real reasons. Though with the way the world had progressed since then, perhaps they weren't as relevant now.

I blinked a couple of times and attempted to chase away the traitorous thoughts swimming through my head. I'd promised Sekhmet I'd do the speed dating in an attempt to make a connection with someone, but she probably didn't intend that person to be my ex.

And nor should it be.

"How are your cats?" he asked.

"They're good. I've gotten more since you last saw me."

"I assumed as much, you never could resist picking up a stray."

"I never heard you complaining about that."

"It was beneficial when I was the stray," he joked.

Despite knowing I shouldn't let him affect me, I melted a little at his words. I had to remember that Ptah was a charmer. It wouldn't just be me he convinced with his sweet talk, it would be every woman he'd talked to so far.

And yet I still felt as if I was the only woman in his world. If I let this continue, then I was doomed to make the same mistakes I already had, and I wasn't sure whether my heart could take it.

I glanced at the man across from me. Perhaps risking my heart would be worth it.

Snag your copy of *Bastet* at your favorite online retailer!

Watch for the other books in the
Speed Dating with the Denizens of the
Underworld Series

Lucifer

Ash

Azrael

Samael

Azazel

Hecate

Bastet

Cain

Thor

Demi

Hell's Belle

Arachne

Osiris

Hades

Adam

HECATE

Loki

Lilith

The Morrígan

Orion

Hera

Abel

Odin

Mormos

Zeus

Michael

Váli

Apollo

Raphael

Baldur

Poseidon

Gabrielle

Frigg

Uriel

And More!

Other Books by Ariel Dawn

The Forevermore Series

In The Cards

In The Blood

In The Shadows

In The Deep

In The Garden

In The Night-coming soon!

Shifters Of Starfall Creek Series

Hollow's Sunrise

Hollow's Sunset

Hollow's Legacy

Get a copy of Ariel Dawn's short story, Faded, when you sign up for her newsletter!

https://mailchi.mp/e5f326e433bf/dawn-breaks-official-newsletter

Where To Find More Of Ariel Dawn

Website

http://www.ariel-dawn.com

Goodreads:

http://www.goodreads.com/authorariel

dawn

Bookbub:

http://www.bookbub.com/authors/ariel

-dawn

Facebook:

http://www.facebook.com/authorarielda

wn

Twitter:

https://twitter.com/ArielDawn10

Join <u>Dusk Chasers—Ariel Dawn's Official Readers Group</u> for access to exclusive content!

ABOUT ARIEL DAWN

USA TODAY BESTSELLING AUTHOR Ariel Dawn grew up as an avid reader and is a creative soul.

What started out as writing reviews for indie romance authors led to featuring quirky, stereotypical, and weird covers on her Instagram Wrong

Turn Romance, which gave her the courage to finally decide to live her dream and become an author.

Ariel writes plot driven paranormal romance and hopes to venture into fantasy and rom-com in the future. When she isn't writing, she can be found cosplaying, attending conventions, creating all sorts of artwork in her studio, or editing photos for her photography business.

A self-professed geek and foodie, she loves hanging out with family and friends and playing video games and board games with her retro gamer husband.

www.ingramcontent.com/pod-product-compliance
Lightning Source LLC
Chambersburg PA
CBHW071432200726
48294CB00002B/604